The Dream of the Butterfly

2

Dreaming a Revolution

CUB
HOUSE

To Yin for her kindness...
To Thomas Ragon for his company and support throughout this process...
To Laurent Duvault who did everything so that The Dream of the Butterfly *could take flight...*
To the entire team at Dargaud who supports our adventures...

To Rachel and Penelope, who are both as guilty of being themselves as Tutu is...
May this adventure teach them something (or not)...

The Dream of the Butterfly, Part 2: Dreaming a Revolution, published 2018 by The Lion Forge, LLC. First published in France under the Original titles: Le Rêve du Papillon 3 - Les Ficelles du cordonnier © DARGAUD 2012, by Marazano, Luo, Le Rêve du Papillon 4 - Hamster au printemps © DARGAUD 2014, by Marazano, Luo, www.dargaud.com. All rights reserved. ROAR™, LION FORGE™, and their associated distinctive designs are trademarks of The Lion Forge, LLC. No similarity between any of the names, characters, persons, and/or institutions in this book with those of any living or dead person or institution is intended and any such similarity which may exist is purely coincidental. Printed in China.

ISBN: 978-1-941302-55-2

Library of Congress Control Number: 2018932762

10 9 8 7 6 5 4 3 2 1

A PROMISE IS A *PROMISE*...

AND THIS *BUTTERFLY* IS VERY IMPORTANT TO ME...

CAPTURE HIM FOR ME, AND I'LL LET YOU GO....

I'LL SACRIFICE A FEW RABBITS TO HELP YOU FIND A PATH OUT OF THE VALLEY....

OF COURSE, I'LL MAKE THEM SWALLOW A *POISON* THAT WILL KILL THEM WHEN THEY RETURN, SO THAT THEY NEVER HAVE A CHANCE TO REVEAL WHAT LIES BEYOND THE MOUNTAINS, BUT YOU'LL BE ON YOUR WAY HOME...

YOU'RE REALLY *TERRIBLE!*

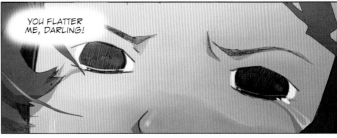

YOU FLATTER ME, DARLING!

I CAN'T....

YES, YOU CAN. YOU'LL SEE....

EVER SINCE I GOT HERE, I'VE BEEN HAVING SOME **STRANGE DREAMS**, AND WHEN I WAKE UP....

NOTHING'S ANY BETTER....

IT'S ALL STILL STRANGE....

TELL ME, DO YOU KNOW HOW TO TELL MY **DREAMS** FROM **REALITY?**

YOU'RE AWFULLY WELL-SPOKEN FOR A LITTLE GIRL....

I'M SURE YOU'LL SUCCEED....

BEYOND YOUR WILDEST DREAMS....

MMM....

ANOTHER ANNOYING DREAM....

ANNOYING AND *DEPRESSING*....

EXCEPT THIS TIME, EVERYTHING WAS COVERED IN SNOW....

AND I COULD STILL HEAR THAT *STUPID EMPEROR'S* VOICE....

HUH....

....WEIRD!

TUTU! DON'T FORGET YOUR BREAKFAST!

UH....WELL....

THAT'S ALRIGHT!

LET'S RECAP...

...THE IDEAL SCHEDULE FOR A LITTLE GIRL TRAPPED IN AN *ENDLESS WINTER*...

AFTER BREAKFAST, MAKE SURE THAT HER *SPIES* ARE HIDING SOMEWHERE NEARBY...

?!

AH, THERE THEY ARE...

GREAT!

DON'T FORGET TO SAY HI TO YOUR FRIEND, *THE TALKING CAT*, SO HE DOESN'T GET *UPSET* THAT YOU FORGOT...

SHHHHHH!

DON'T CRY IF YOU DON'T THINK YOU CAN TRUST ANYONE HERE...

≥SIGH≤

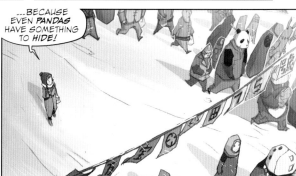

...BECAUSE EVEN *PANDAS* HAVE SOMETHING TO *HIDE*!

UUUGHH...

!!!

HEY! IT'S NOT VERY NICE TO PRETEND LIKE YOU DON'T EVEN KNOW ME! EVEN IF YOU DON'T TRUST ME, YOU COULD AT LEAST BE POLITE ABOUT IT!

HMMPH.... EXCUSE ME....

STRANGE THINGS HAVE BEEN HAPPENING FOR SOME TIME NOW....

THE *EMPEROR* IS PREPARING FOR SOMETHING.... IF YOU REALLY WANT TO *HELP US,* MAYBE I COULD....

I KNOW, WE NEED TO BE *DISCRETE*... STEP BACK, SOMEONE MIGHT *HEAR* US.

Tooooot!

YOU'RE REALLY *SOMETHING!*

...

?!

YOU?!

YOU SHOULDN'T BE HERE!

IF THE OTHERS FIND YOU...

NO! WAIT! DON'T GO! I CAN HELP YOU!

YOU KNOW THAT A BUNCH OF PEOPLE ARE LOOKING FOR YOU...OOPS! I DON'T KNOW WHAT THEY WANT WITH YOU, BUT DON'T WORRY...

I'M NOT GOING TO GIVE YOU UP THAT EASILY!

WE'RE THE SAME, YOU AND ME...

THERE! LET ME GET JUST A LITTLE CLOSER...

YOU *TRUST ME*, RIGHT?

HEY!

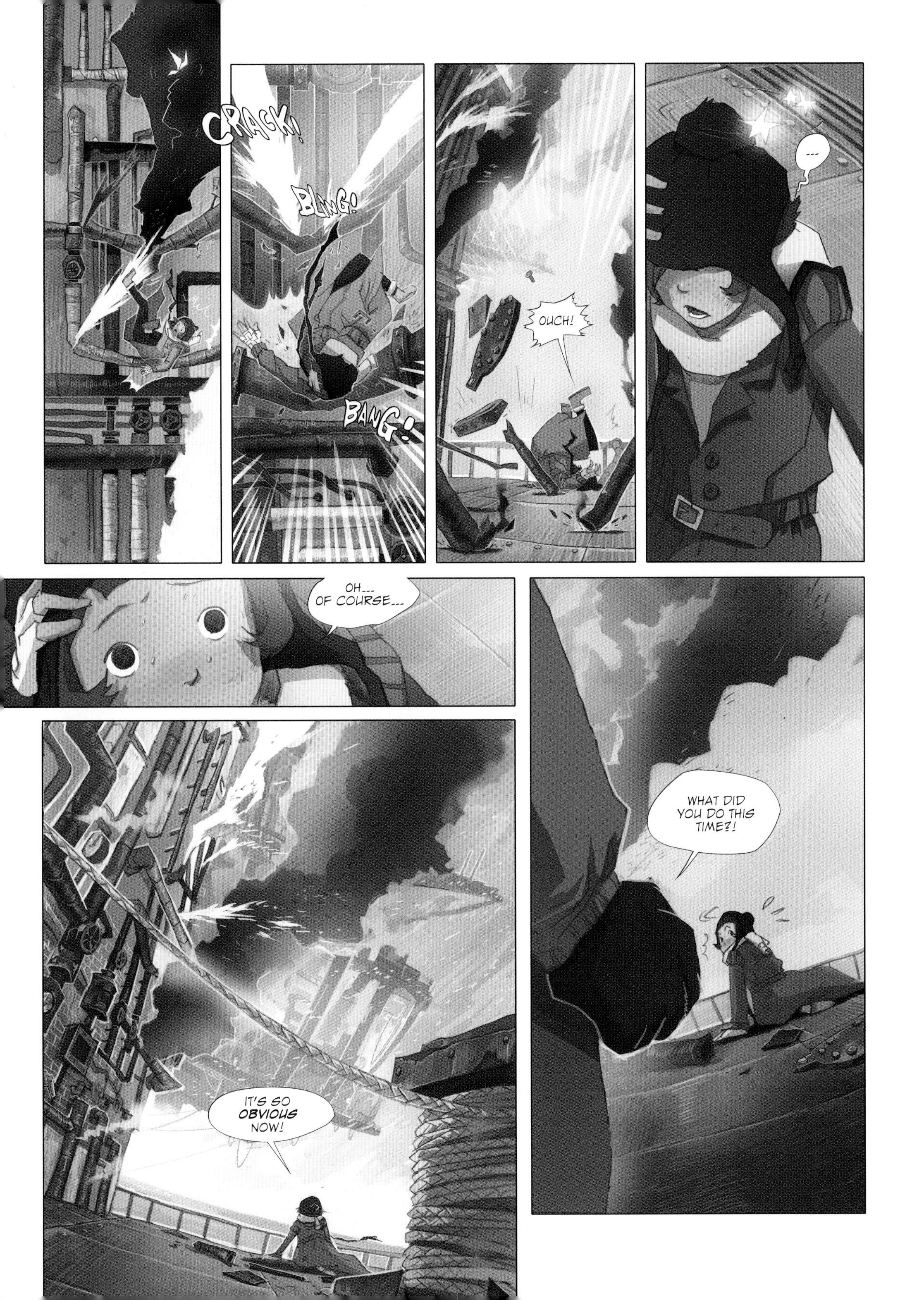
CRACK!
BLING!
BANG!
OUCH!
...
OH...
OF COURSE...
IT'S SO
OBVIOUS
NOW!
WHAT DID
YOU DO THIS
TIME?!

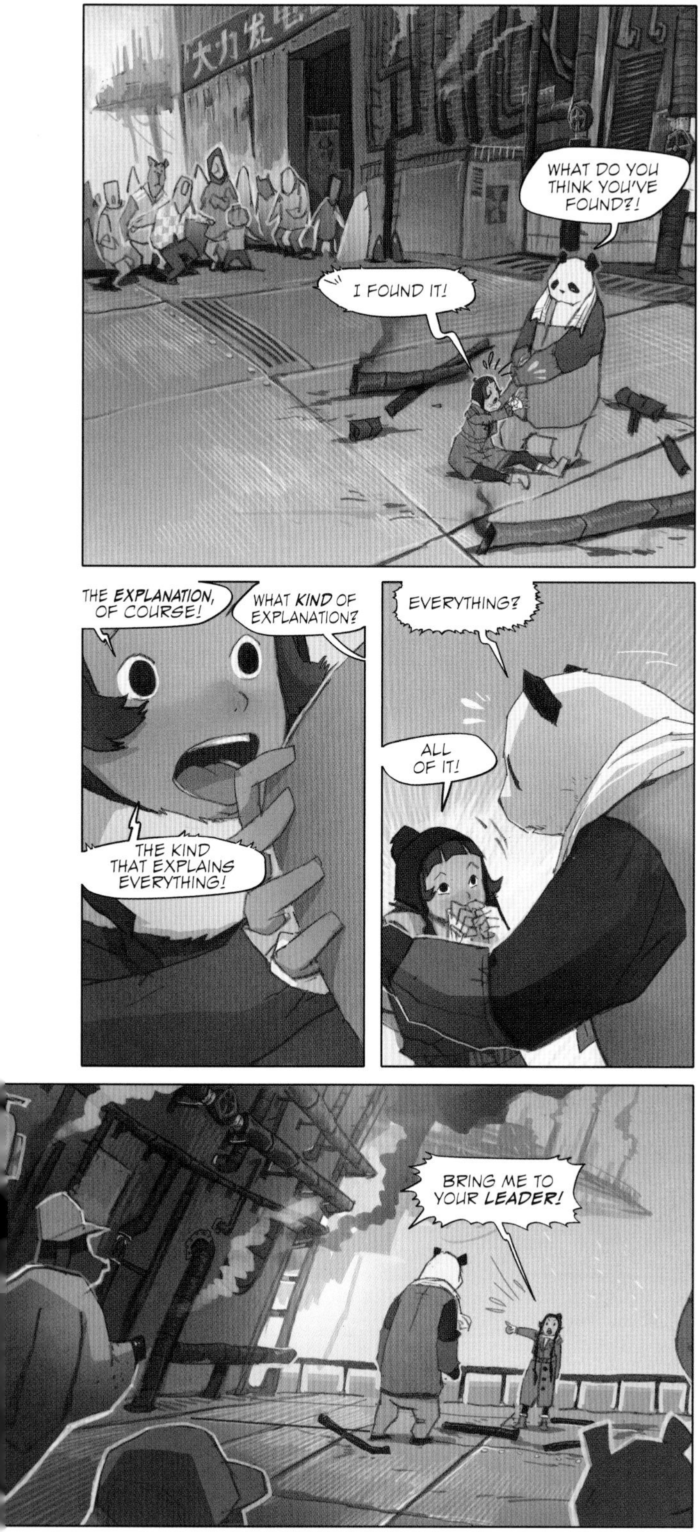
WHAT DO YOU THINK YOU'VE FOUND?!
I FOUND IT!
THE **EXPLANATION**, OF COURSE!
WHAT **KIND** OF EXPLANATION?
THE KIND THAT EXPLAINS EVERYTHING!
EVERYTHING?
ALL OF IT!
BRING ME TO YOUR **LEADER!**

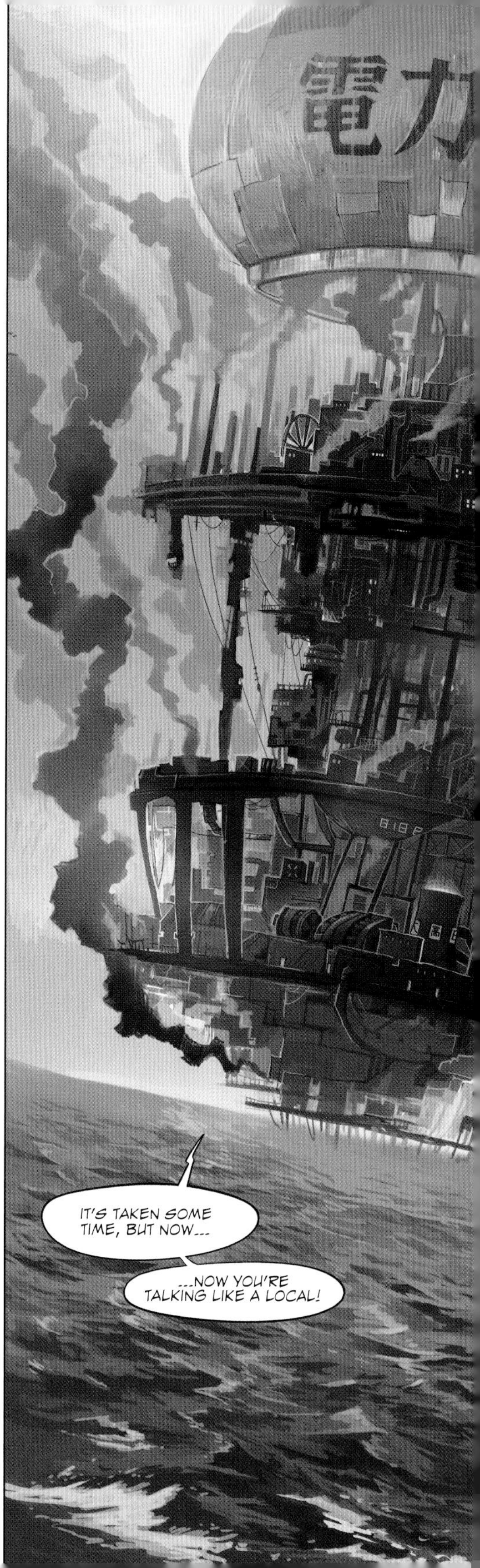
電力
IT'S TAKEN SOME TIME, BUT NOW...
...NOW YOU'RE TALKING LIKE A LOCAL!

IT'S SIMPLE ENOUGH, YOU'LL SEE...

THE REASON FOR YOUR *SERVITUDE* IS THESE *FACTORIES*, RIGHT?!

BUT, AT THE SAME TIME, YOU'RE WORRIED ABOUT HOW YOUR VALLEY IS SLOWLY *FREEZING,* SO YOU FEEL RESPONSIBLE FOR THE WORK YOU DO HERE TO PRODUCE THE *HEAT.*

BUT THAT'S WHERE YOU'RE *WRONG!*

HAHAHA!

YOU'LL SEE, I'M REALLY QUITE CLEVER; I FIGURED IT OUT ALL BY MYSELF...

THE *SMOKE* FROM THE FACTORY IS CAUSING THE *CLOUDS* THAT COVER THE VALLEY AND STOP THE SUN FROM PIERCING THROUGH!

THIS KID IS REALLY CLEVER, ISN'T SHE?!

QUITE! IT TOOK HER ALL THIS TIME JUST TO FIGURE OUT WHAT WE'VE KNOWN FOR YEARS...

THAT'S WHY IT'S SO *COLD* HERE! THE *FACTORIES* AREN'T THE *SOLUTION;* THEY'RE THE *PROBLEM!*

HOW? YOU... YOU ALREADY KNEW?

YES, BUT OUR **PROBLEM** IS FINDING A WAY TO GET **RID** OF THE EMPEROR.... HE'S THE ONE WHO FORCES US TO WORK....

YEAH! HE CONTROLS **EVERYTHING!** AND EVERYONE KEEPS SAYING THERE'S NO OTHER WAY.

SO, EVENTUALLY, THE PEOPLE IN THE VALLEY START TO **BELIEVE** HIM!

YEAH. AND BESIDES, WHAT KIND OF **WORK** WOULD WE EVEN DO?! ALL WE KNOW HOW TO DO IS WORK IN THIS FACTORY!

AS LONG AS THE EMPEROR IS STILL AROUND, WE CAN'T CHANGE ANYTHING!

AND HE HAS SPIES. HE MUST KNOW WHAT WE'RE UP TO. BUT WE HAVE NO IDEA WHAT HE'S PLANNING....

IF YOU REALLY WANT TO HELP US, YOU CAN **FIND OUT**....

AWW MAN, AND HERE I WAS THINKING I HAD FIGURED EVERYTHING OUT!

?!

WELL.... ALMOST EVERYTHING....

WHAT? A *LIBRARY?*

YES, A LIBRARY! WHAT? YOU'RE GOING TO TELL ME THERE'S NOT A SINGLE *LIBRARY* IN THE ENTIRE VALLEY?

YES...THERE IS A LIBRARY, BUT....

BUT WHAT?!

BUT THERE'S NOT MUCH CHANCE THAT *LITTLE GIRLS* WOULD BE *ALLOWED* THERE...

REALLY? AND WHY WOULD THAT BE, MISTER *RABBIT?!*

ACTUALLY, *NOBODY* IN THE VALLEY READS.

WHAT? YOU NEVER READ? BUT....BUT WHY?!

I DON'T KNOW...THEY COULD GET SOME WEIRD *IDEAS,* FROM ALL THOSE *BOOKS*...

WELL...MAYBE IT COULD GIVE US SOME WEIRD IDEAS, TOO...

YOU'RE GOING TO FIND A WAY FOR ME TO GET *INTO* THAT LIBRARY!

YOU'RE GOING TO END UP GETTING US IN **TROUBLE**...

IF YOU JUST CAME TO COMPLAIN, YOU SHOULD'VE STAYED BEHIND.

BUT YOU DIDN'T GIVE US A **CHOICE**. YOU SAID YOU WOULD TELL THE EMPEROR THAT WE ATE ALL OF HIS FROZEN RICE BALLS...

SO, YOU DID IT, DIDN'T YOU?!

YES, BUT IT WAS A **SECRET**! AND YOU PROMISED NOT TO SAY ANYTHING! WE SHOULDN'T HAVE **TRUSTED** YOU...

HAHAHA! YOU SHOULD NEVER TRUST A **LITTLE GIRL**!

ISN'T THAT WHAT YOU ALWAYS SAY?!

RIGHTFULLY SO!

ALWAYS SO **PREJUDICED**...

IS THE LIBRARY MUCH FARTHER?

NO, NO. WE'RE THERE...

YOU WON'T BE DISAPPOINTED...

ISN'T IT? APPARENTLY THE EMPEROR SPENT HIS YOUTH IN HERE, READING ALL OF THESE BOOKS!

INCREDIBLE!

ALL OF THEM? BUT THIS LIBRARY IS *HUGE!* IT'S SUCH A *SHAME* YOU DON'T HAVE THE RIGHT TO READ...

WHO SAID WE DIDN'T HAVE THE RIGHT? WE KNOW WHAT WE'RE ALLOWED AND *NOT* ALLOWED TO *DO!*

OH? BUT I THOUGHT...

SO, NO PROBLEM THEN? YOU CAN HELP ME CHOOSE!

MAYBE THIS ONE?

UHH, THIS FEELS SO WEIRD...

NO, NO, NOT LIKE THAT! YOU'RE GOING TO FIND AND BRING ME ALL THE BOOKS THAT MENTION *BUTTERFLIES...*

?

WE'RE GETTING ROPED INTO ANOTHER OF HER *PLANS;* I'M GETTING THAT *FEELING...*

OH REALLY? WHAT KIND OF FEELING?

A VERY NICE ONE, ACTUALLY! HEH...

I NEVER WOULD'VE IMAGINED THE NUMBER OF BOOKS ABOUT BUTTERFLIES!

BUTTERFLIES!

BUTTERFLIES!

IT'S TOO BAD THEY DON'T EXIST, THEY'RE ACTUALLY QUITE CUTE!

I AGREE! THEY'RE SO... FLIGHTY...

BUTTERFLIES AREN'T MYTHOLOGICAL! THEY ACTUALLY EXIST!

BECAUSE THEY ONLY COME DURING SPRINGTIME, AND YOU, YOU STUPID RABBITS, LIVE IN AN ETERNAL WINTER!

OH, REALLY? AND WHY HAVE WE NEVER SEEN ANY, THEN?

LIKE I WAS SAYING. THEY DON'T EXIST! JUST LIKE SPRING...

NO, SPRING EXISTS, TOO!

SHE'S FULL OF IT!

SILLY!

COMPLETELY ABSURD!

THAT'S ENOUGH!

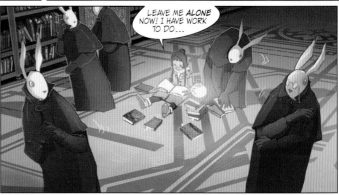

LEAVE ME ALONE NOW! I HAVE WORK TO DO...

BUTTERFLY... BUTTERFLY...

"THE BUTTERFLY IS A SWIMMING STROKE PERFORMED WITH BOTH ARMS MOVING SYMMETRICALLY, ACCOMPANIED BY A...."

NO.... THAT'S NOT IT....

AND HERE? "THE BUTTERFLY IS A VALVE THAT ISOLATES OR REGULATES THE FLOW OF A FLUID."

PFF... WHAT'S THE POINT OF HAVING RABBITS THAT MOVE SO QUICKLY TO FIND SUCH USELESS INFORMATION...

OH, HERE WE GO...

"LEPIDOPTERA... AN ORDER OF INSECTS WHOSE ADULT FORM ARE COMMONLY CALLED BUTTERFLIES!"

HM....

"BUTTERFLY SYMBOLISM: FOR SOME, THE BUTTERFLIES REPRESENT IMMORTALITY, FOR OTHERS, METAMORPHOSIS, OR CHANGE...

...LOVE, OR EVEN THE SOUL OF INNOCENCE, FINALLY FREE..."

"AN ANCIENT PEOPLE (THE MAYANS) CALLED IT 'HUNAB KU' AND SAW IT AS THE SOUL OF THE WORLD...."

MMM.... THIS IS ALL SO COMPLICATED. I NEVER IMAGINED THAT BUTTERFLIES COULD BE SUCH A DIFFICULT SUBJECT...

HUH, WHAT'S THIS?

THE BUTTERFLY...

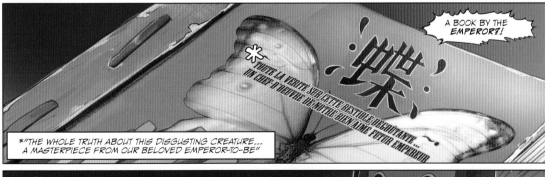

A BOOK BY THE EMPEROR?!

蝶

* TOUTE LA VERITÉ SUR CETTE BESTIOLE DÉGOUTANTE... UN CHEF-D'OEUVRE DE NOTRE BIEN-AIMÉ FUTUR EMPEREUR

*"THE WHOLE TRUTH ABOUT THIS DISGUSTING CREATURE.... A MASTERPIECE FROM OUR BELOVED EMPEROR-TO-BE"

?!

CRACK!

CROOOOCCC...

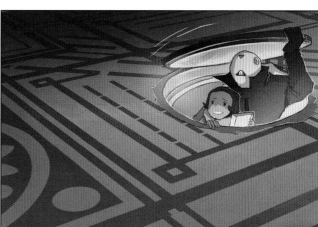

TAP!

TAP!

TAP!

PSHHHH...

GUESS MY HOST ISN'T SO BAD AFTER ALL...

JUST HAVE TO AVOID WONDERING WHAT'S ACTUALLY *INSIDE*...

WHAT ARE YOU HIDING UNDER THERE?

OH! IT'S YOU! IT'S NOTHING, JUST SOME *BISCUITS* IN CASE I'M HUNGRY LATER...

I THINK THEY'RE CALLED *CAT TONGUES*...

YOU WANT ONE?

CAT TONGUES?! *BLEH!* HOW TERRIBLE!

YOU WOULDN'T BE *HIDING* SOMETHING FROM ME, WOULD YOU?

WE'LL HAVE TO BE MORE *CAREFUL...*

EVERYTHING SEEMS SO *UNCERTAIN* SINCE SHE ARRIVED HERE.

WE'LL HAVE TO BE MORE CAREFUL...

THE *EMPEROR* MUST BE ON GUARD BY NOW...

THAT'S QUITE POSSIBLE, DEAR...

AND I DON'T KNOW IF WE CAN *TRUST* THAT LITTLE *GIRL...*

WE'LL HAVE TO BE MORE CAREFUL...

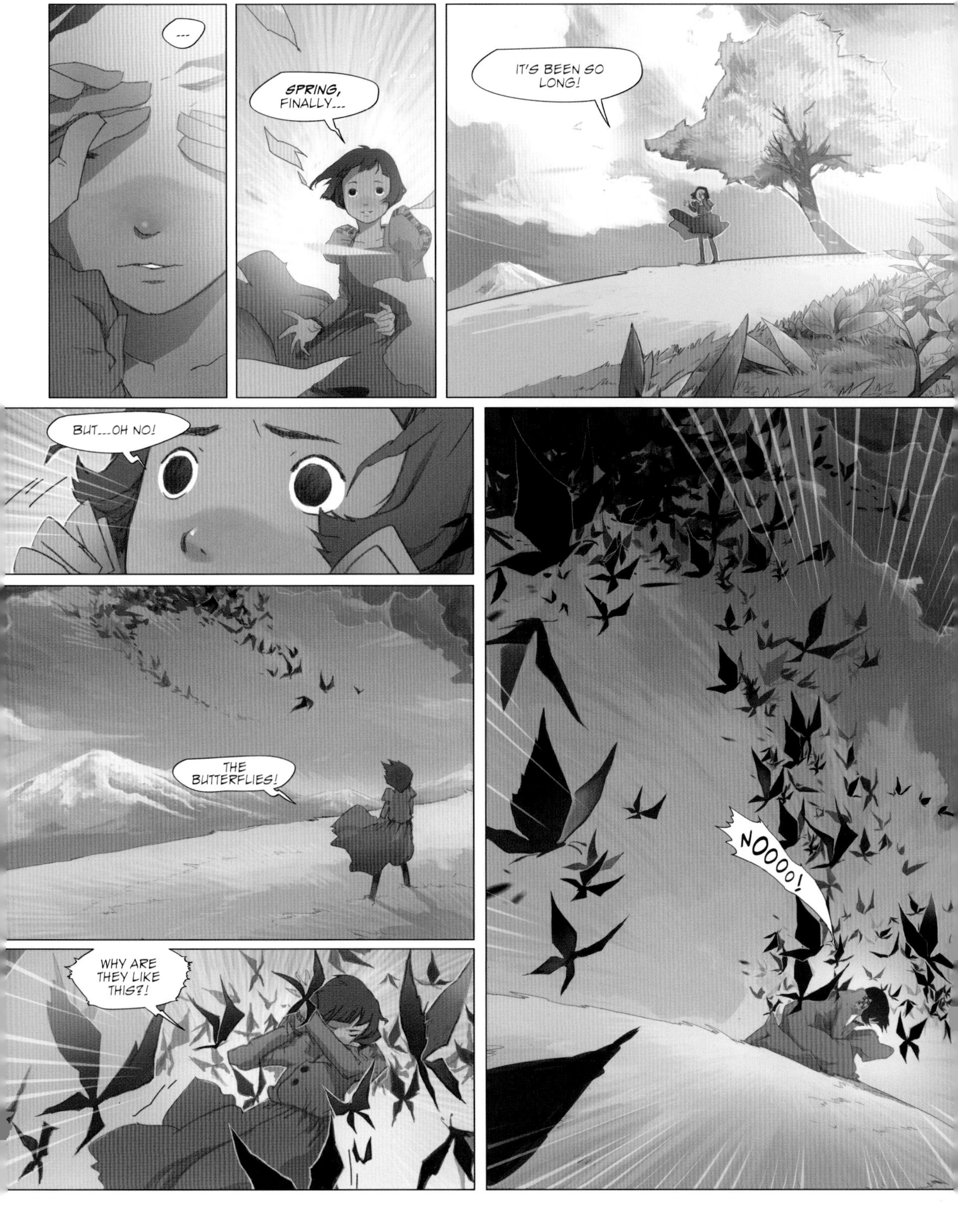
...
SPRING, FINALLY...
IT'S BEEN SO LONG!
BUT...OH NO!
THE BUTTERFLIES!
WHY ARE THEY LIKE THIS?!
NOOOO!

AHHHH!

WHAT AN AWFUL *NIGHTMARE*. I LIKED IT BETTER WHEN IT WAS STILL *WINTER*, WHEN THE BUTTERFLIES WERE STILL...

IT'S A LITTLE SCARY, BUT I CAN'T HELP BUT FEEL THAT THIS *BOOK* HOLDS THE KEY TO THE *MYSTERY* OF THE *EMPEROR* AND THAT *STRANGE BUTTERFLY*...

HMM....MUST BE THIS AWFUL BOOK!

BUT... WHERE?

I KNEW YOU WERE HIDING SOMETHING!

Y-YOU? BUT YOU NEVER COME IN THE MORNING!

IT CAN BE *USEFUL* TO *CHANGE* YOUR HABITS, FROM TIME TO TIME....AS I'VE SHOWN YOU!

HEY, DON'T TAKE THAT TONE WITH ME! YOU'VE BEEN HIDING THINGS FROM ME SINCE THE *BEGINNING!*

THAT'S NOT THE SAME! WE'RE DOING THAT FOR YOUR OWN GOOD!

TYRANTS ALWAYS WANT TO PROTECT PEOPLE FROM THEMSELVES FOR THEIR OWN GOOD!

I'M TIRED OF EVERYONE THINKING THEY KNOW WHAT'S BEST FOR ME BETTER THAN *I* DO!

HEY!

TUTU! COME BACK!

A LITTLE GIRL BEING **CHASED** BY A CAT? YOU DON'T SEE THAT EVERY DAY...

YEAH....SHOULDN'T IT BE THE OTHER WAY AROUND?

YOUNG PEOPLE THESE DAYS. THEY JUST DON'T RESPECT ANYTHING ANYMORE!

IN MY DAY....

TUTU! COME BACK HERE!

OOPS!

OH NO....

WHAT? WHAT'S GOING ON?

COME HERE, TUTU, YOU CAN'T STAY THERE....THOSE ARE.... THOSE ARE **GHOSTS!**

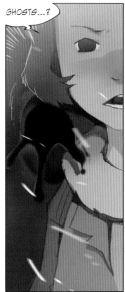

GHOSTS....?

!!

WELL, IF YOU HAVE TO KNOW, THEY'RE NOT REALLY GHOSTS... BUT THAT'S WHAT WE CALL THEM... CAN YOU GIVE ME THE BOOK NOW?

UH...IF THEY'RE NOT GHOSTS, THEN WHAT ARE THEY?!

PEOPLE SAY THEY'RE THE OLD FACTORY WORKERS!

DON'T SCREAM! YOU'LL MAKE THEM *ANGRY*, AND WE DON'T KNOW WHAT THEY'LL DO IF THEY GET...

...THE *KIDS* WHO USED TO WORK THERE!

WHAT?!

GIVE ME THE BOOK, PLEASE!

NO WAY!

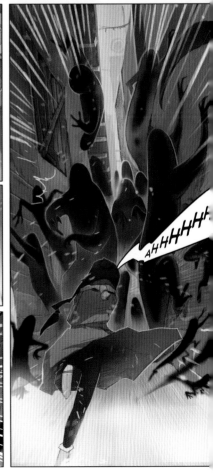

AHHHHH!

NOOOOO!

AHHHHH!

BRR...

...SO COLD!

SHHHH!

AAAH!

SHE MADE IT THROUGH... I REALLY CAN'T STAND THAT GIRL!

YOU DIDN'T NEED TO CHASE HER. YOU MADE HER TAKE A BIG RISK!

WHEN WE BOTH ALREADY KNOW WHAT'S IN THAT BOOK...

AND, SOON, SHE'LL KNOW, TOO!

≶HFFF≶
≶HFF≶

≶HFFF≶

THOSE POOR
PEOPLE...

BRRR...

BUMP!

PLOF!

?

OF COURSE!
HOW DID I NOT
THINK OF IT
BEFORE?

I'LL SHOW
HIM WHAT I'M
MADE OF!

LET'S GO!

BLAAM!
BLAAM!
BLAAM!

YOU'RE GOING TO OPEN THIS DOOR! YOU...

KBLIXT KKKKTXT!

OPEN UP! OR I'LL BREAK DOWN THE DOOR!

BLAAM!

BLAAM!

LET HER IN, MAXIME! SHE'S PERFECTLY CAPABLE OF ACTING ON HER THREAT JUST TO EMBARRASS US.

AND WE WOULDN'T WANT HER TO INJURE OUR REPUTATION, WOULD WE?

YOUR REPUTATION?!

YOUR REPUTATION?!

YOU POOR, UNFORTUNATE MAN. YOUR REPUTATION CAN'T SINK ANY LOWER!

BUT...BUT WAIT, WHAT ARE YOU...

NOW, MOVE! I WANT TO SEE THE EMPEROR'S REAL FACE!

CRSSHHH!

WHAT A PEST!

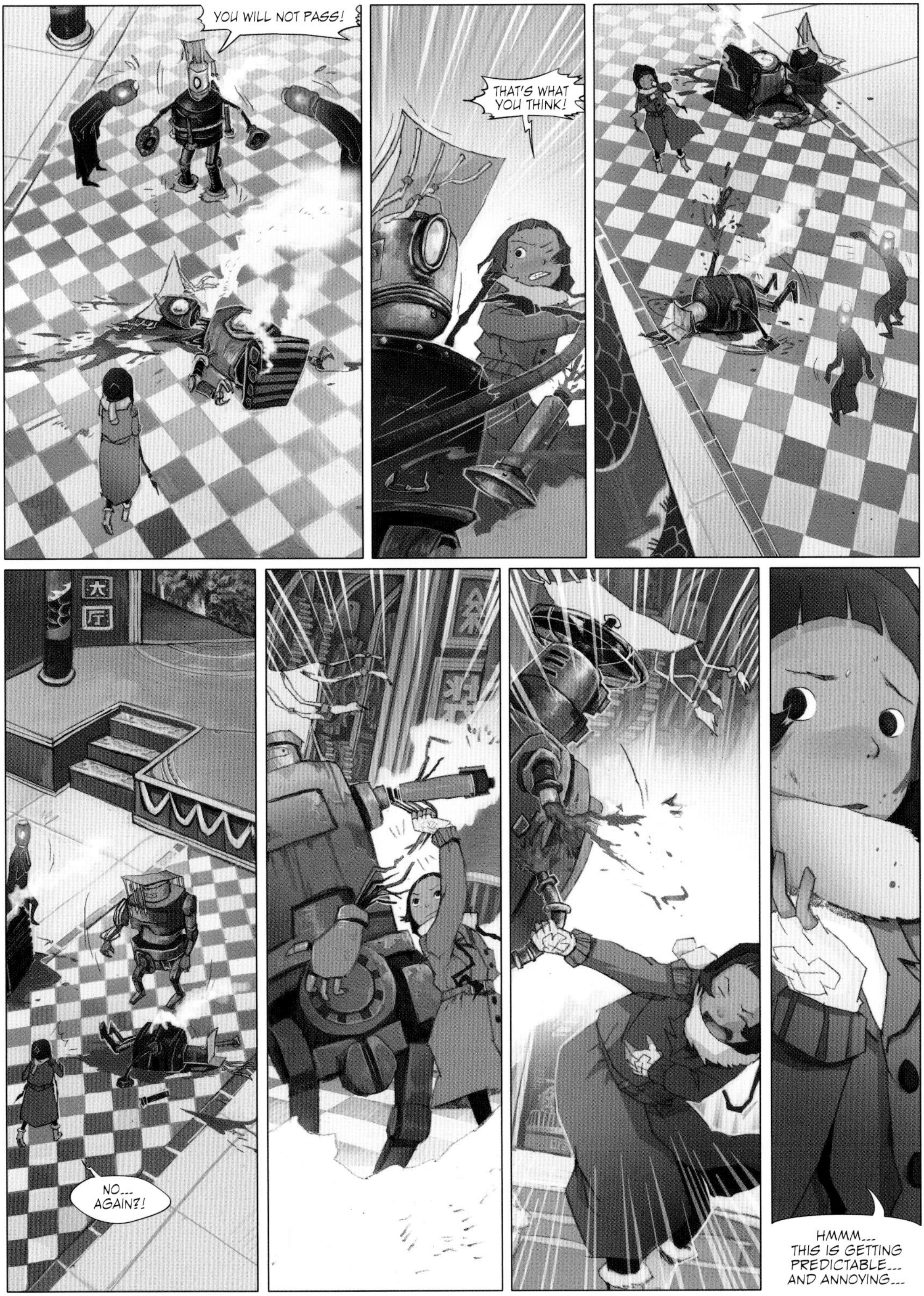
YOU WILL NOT PASS!
THAT'S WHAT YOU THINK!
NO... AGAIN?!
HMMM... THIS IS GETTING PREDICTABLE... AND ANNOYING...

CRACK!
CRACK!

WHAT A MESS...

?!

SO? IS THAT ALL YOU'VE GOT?

OH! OH! LOOK AT ME, I'M A PATHETIC EMPEROR OF JUNK AND BROKEN ROBOTS!

HAHAHA!

OH!

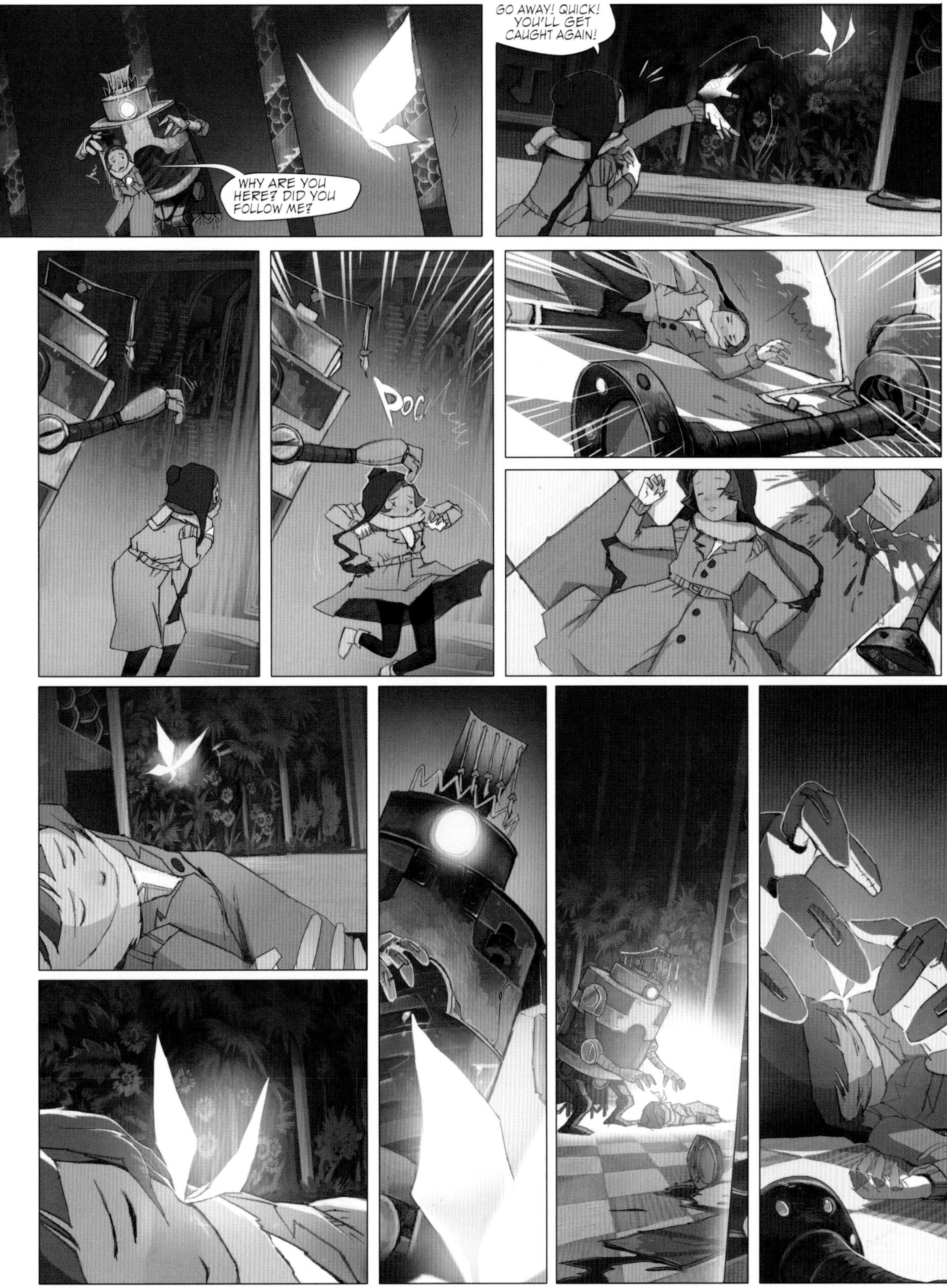
WHY ARE YOU HERE? DID YOU FOLLOW ME?
GO AWAY! QUICK! YOU'LL GET CAUGHT AGAIN!
POC!

?!

THAT'S IMPOSSIBLE!

BUT...
BUT?

I...I'M A BUTTERFLY!

?!

THESE DREAMS... THEY JUST KEEP GETTING WEIRDER...

YOUR MAJESTY, THE LITTLE ONE IS WAKING UP!

MY POOR CHILD, YOU'RE REALLY A LOST CAUSE...

TSSS! TSSS!

?!

WHAT ARE YOU GOING TO DO WITH ME?

NOTHING, MY DEAR, DON'T WORRY...

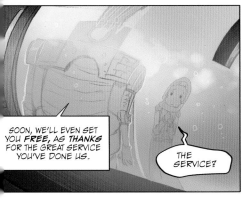

SOON, WE'LL EVEN SET YOU FREE, AS THANKS FOR THE GREAT SERVICE YOU'VE DONE US.

THE SERVICE?

LOOK FOR YOURSELF...

?!

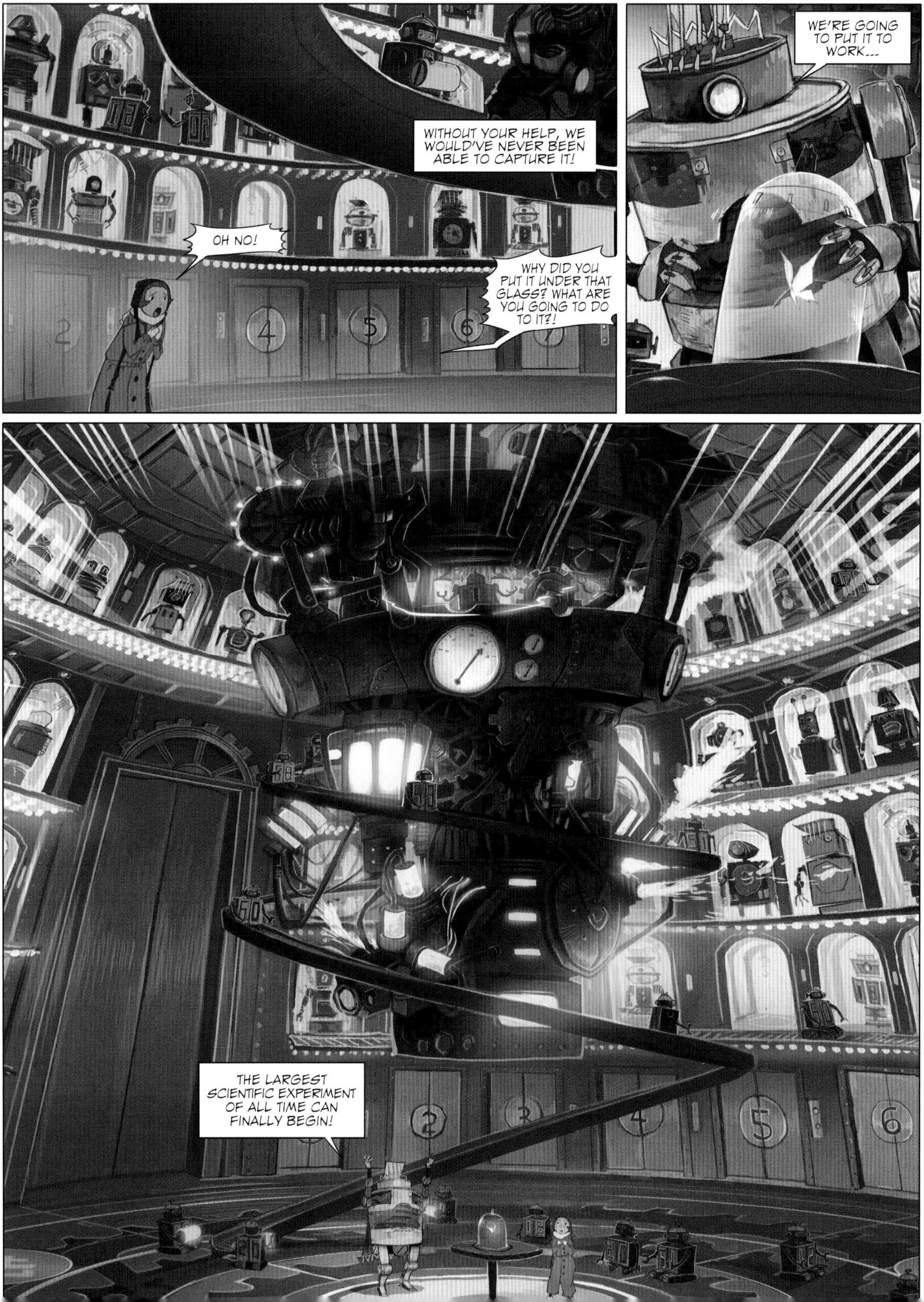
WITHOUT YOUR HELP, WE WOULD'VE NEVER BEEN ABLE TO CAPTURE IT!
OH NO!
WHY DID YOU PUT IT UNDER THAT GLASS? WHAT ARE YOU GOING TO DO TO IT?!
WE'RE GOING TO PUT IT TO WORK...
THE LARGEST SCIENTIFIC EXPERIMENT OF ALL TIME CAN FINALLY BEGIN!

I KNOW WHO YOU ARE, AND I KNOW WHY YOU *HATE* THE *BUTTERFLIES* SO MUCH!

YOU DON'T KNOW ANYTHING! YOU'RE JUST A *PRESUMPTUOUS*, *DISHONEST* LITTLE GIRL...

I COULD GET RID OF YOU EASILY!

BUT YOU WON'T! BECAUSE YOUR CUTE LITTLE SPIES WOULDN'T LET YOU TREAT ME LIKE THAT!

WHEN THE PEOPLE IN THE VALLEY FIND OUT WHO YOU *REALLY* ARE, YOU WON'T SCARE *ANYONE*.

MAYBE, BUT... WHO WILL TELL THEM?

...

WHEN ALL THIS IS *OVER*, YOU WILL BE *BANISHED* FROM THE VALLEY! AND THE ORDER OF THINGS WILL BE MORE.... ORDERLY!

MMM MMM MMM

ZAP

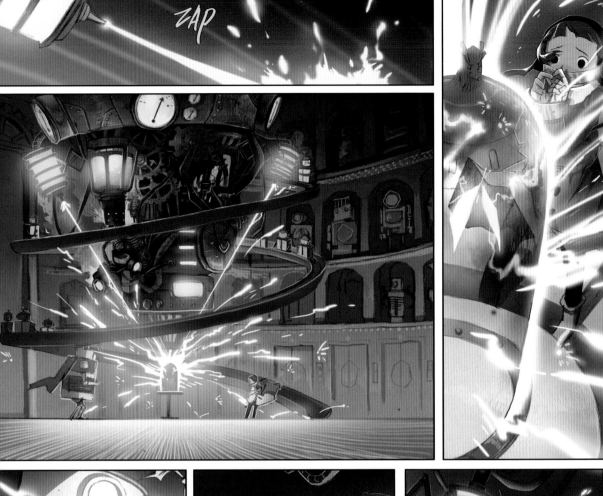

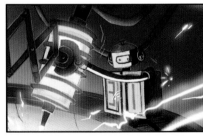

CLAP CLAP

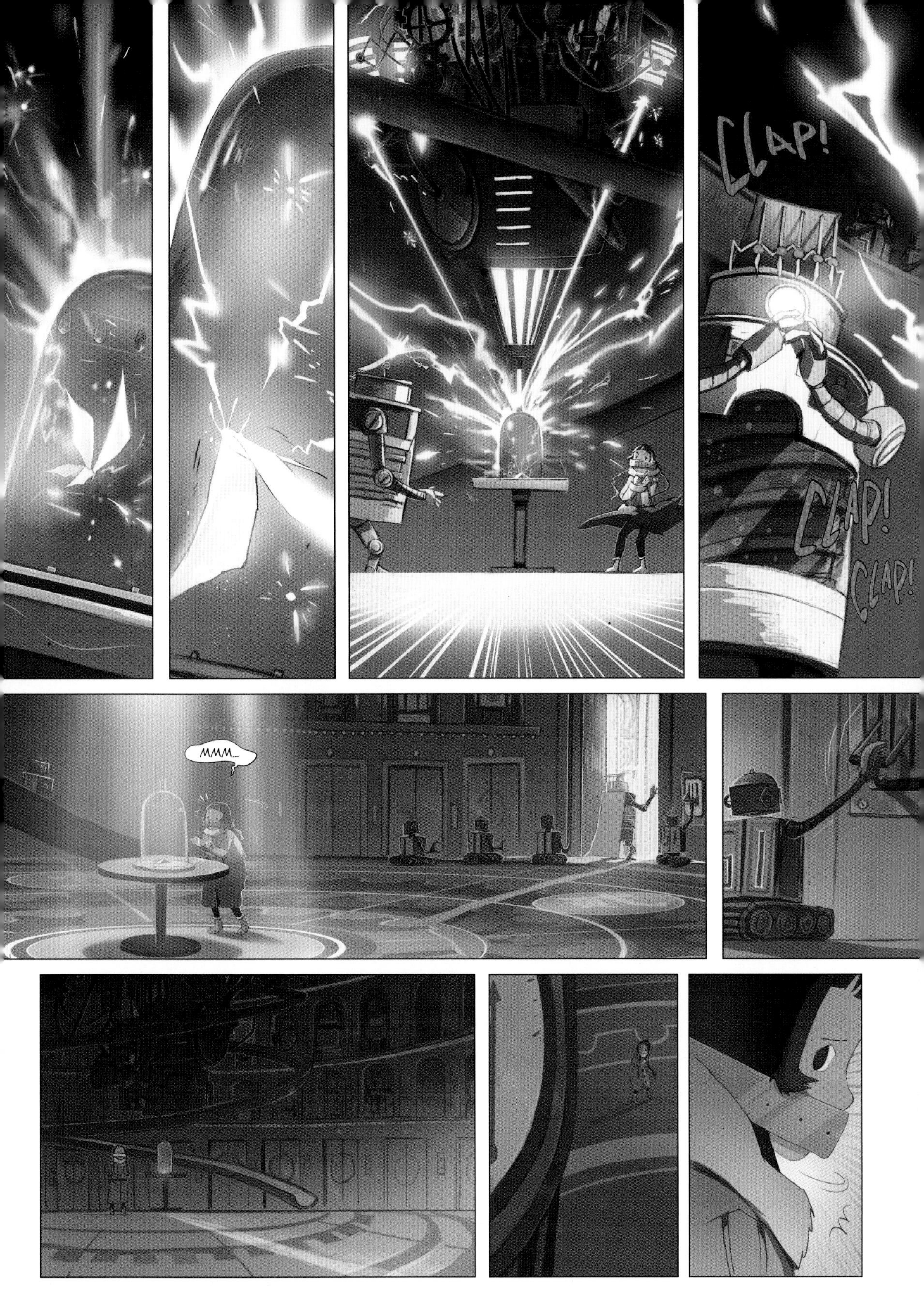
CLAP!
CLAP!
CLAP!
MMM...

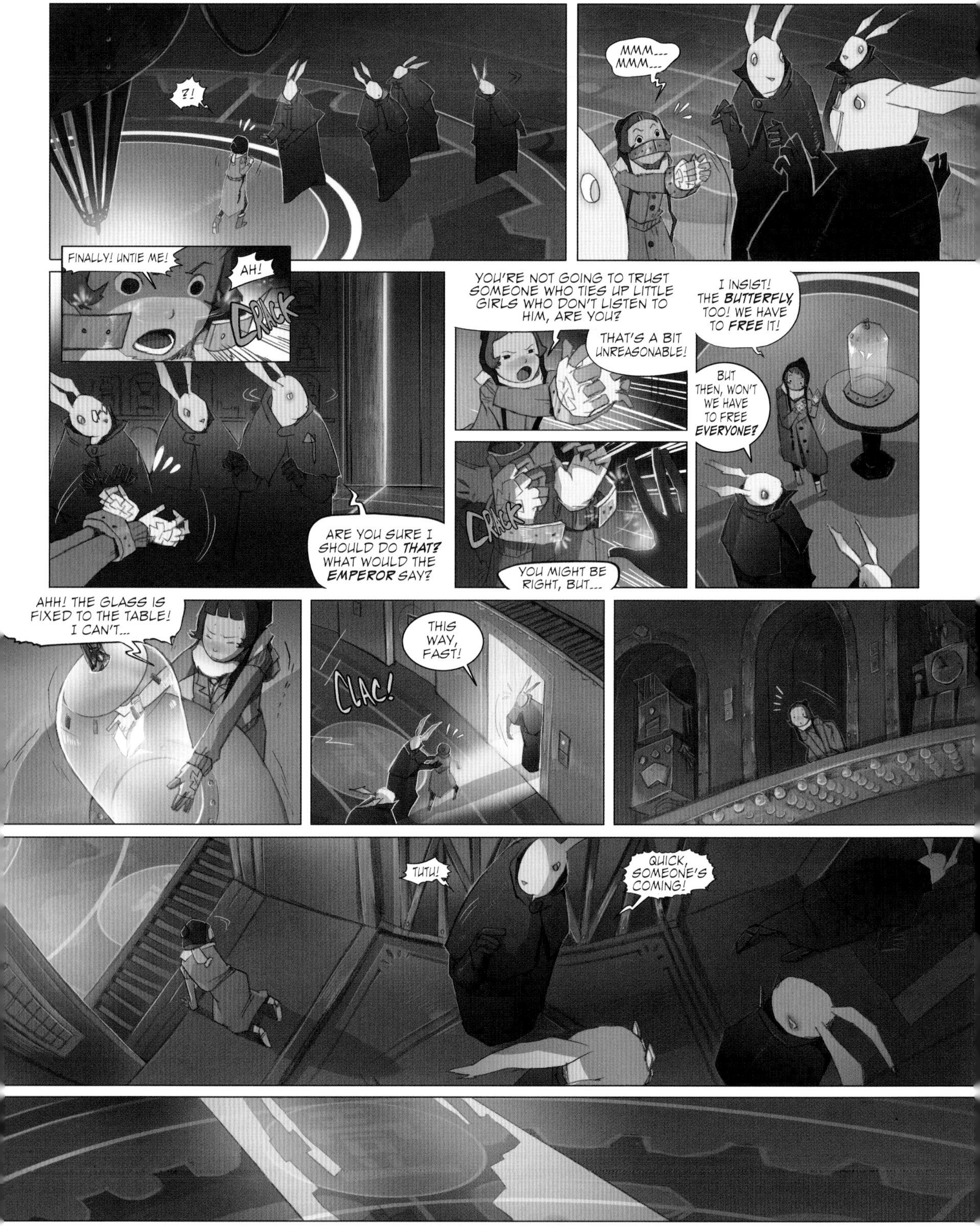
?!
MMM...
MMM...
FINALLY! UNTIE ME!
AH!
CRACK
ARE YOU SURE I SHOULD DO THAT? WHAT WOULD THE EMPEROR SAY?
YOU'RE NOT GOING TO TRUST SOMEONE WHO TIES UP LITTLE GIRLS WHO DON'T LISTEN TO HIM, ARE YOU?
THAT'S A BIT UNREASONABLE!
CRACK
YOU MIGHT BE RIGHT, BUT...
I INSIST! THE BUTTERFLY, TOO! WE HAVE TO FREE IT!
BUT THEN, WON'T WE HAVE TO FREE EVERYONE?
AHH! THE GLASS IS FIXED TO THE TABLE! I CAN'T...
CLAC!
THIS WAY, FAST!
TUTU!
QUICK, SOMEONE'S COMING!

BE CAREFUL, MISS TUTU...

OOOH....

WHAT'S GOING ON? ARE YOU FEELING OKAY?

NO, I'M OKAY, BUT....I JUST *UNDERSTOOD*...

EVERYTHING IS MY *FAULT*!

WHAT'S YOUR FAULT?

ALL OF THIS! CAN'T YOU SEE THAT THE EMPEROR USED ME?!

HE USED ME FROM THE *BEGINNING* TO CATCH THAT *BUTTERFLY*, AND WHO KNOWS WHAT ELSE!

OH! THAT? HE'S BEEN USING US LIKE THAT FOR A LONG TIME... BUT WHAT CAN WE DO?

DON'T YOU WANT TO *REBEL*? TO JUST BREAK OUT?

SOMETIMES YES... BUT WE'RE *RABBITS*, YOU KNOW, WE DON'T HAVE THE *TEMPERAMENT* FOR SUCH THINGS...

I THINK WE ALL UNDERESTIMATED THE *INTENTIONS* OF THAT DIABOLICAL *EMPEROR*!

WHAT NOW?

WHERE AM I?

IS SOMEONE HERE?

?!

WHAT... WHAT IS THIS?

THE GLASS?! WHY AM I UNDER THE GLASS NOW?!

OF COURSE! HOW COULD WE BEGIN THE *EXPERIMENT* WITHOUT YOU?

AN *EXPERIMENT?* ON ME? NO WAY!

NOW, NOW, TUTU... DON'T MAKE A BIG DEAL OUT OF THIS...WHERE ELSE DO YOU WANT US TO FIND A *BUTTERFLY* THIS TIME OF YEAR?

AAAAAHH!

ARE YOU OKAY, MISS TUTU?

WHY ARE YOU SCREAMING? DID YOU HAVE A NIGHTMARE?

WHERE ARE WE?

HIDING IN THE SEWERS...YOU FELL *ASLEEP* AND YOU KEPT REPEATING, "I'M NOT A *BUTTERFLY!* I'M NOT A *BUTTERFLY!*"

BUT IT'S *TRUE!* I'M NOT A *BUTTERFLY!*

OF COURSE NOT...BUT THINKING ABOUT THE BUTTERFLY IN THE STORY MAKES YOU *SAD*, DOESN'T IT?

AND IT'S KIND OF *OUR* FAULT....

NO, NO...I SHOULD BE *THANKING* YOU FOR GETTING ME OUT OF THERE....

YOU'RE TAKING A *BIG RISK* FOR ME....

BUT WE SHOULD'VE BROUGHT THAT *BUTTERFLY* WITH US....

YES....

?!

...YOU SHOULD'VE!

AAAAAAHHH!

REALLY, MISS TUTU....
DON'T YOU HAVE ANY WAY OF
CALMING THEM DOWN?

AAHHH!

AAAHHH...

PUT YOURSELF IN THEIR PLACE. THEY'VE
BEEN TRYING TO *CAPTURE* YOU ALL THIS
TIME, AND ALL OF A SUDDEN, THEY TURN
AROUND AND FIND THEMSELVES AT
YOUR *MERCY*....

IT'S A BIT OF A SHOCK TO
THEM, ESPECIALLY WHEN THEY'RE SO
FRAGILE...BECAUSE OF EVERYTHING
THEY'VE DONE FOR ME.

IT'S JUST....
THEY'RE SO
LOUD!

AAHHH!

...

AAAHHH!!!
AAHHH!

YOU'RE NOT WRONG....

HMM....

EXCUSE ME, MISTER
RABBITS, BUT MAYBE YOU
COULD STOP RUNNING AND
SCREAMING? THE *FLYING BANDIT*
HAS BEEN STANDING WITH
US FOR A WHILE NOW AND
HE HASN'T TRIED TO
HURT YOU....

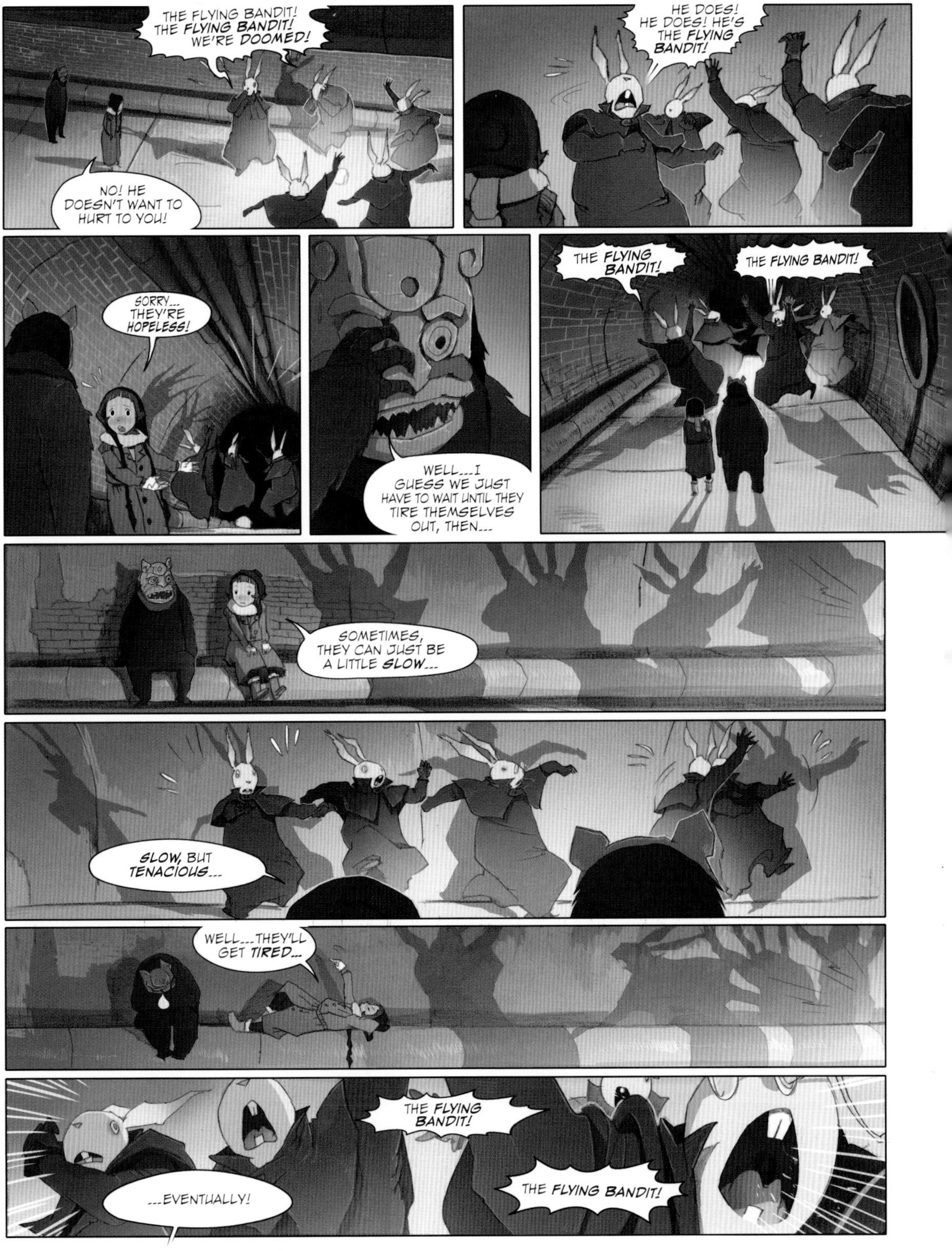
THE FLYING BANDIT! THE FLYING BANDIT! WE'RE DOOMED!
NO! HE DOESN'T WANT TO HURT TO YOU!
HE DOES! HE DOES! HE'S THE FLYING BANDIT!
SORRY... THEY'RE HOPELESS!
WELL... I GUESS WE JUST HAVE TO WAIT UNTIL THEY TIRE THEMSELVES OUT, THEN...
THE FLYING BANDIT!
THE FLYING BANDIT!
SOMETIMES, THEY CAN JUST BE A LITTLE SLOW...
SLOW, BUT TENACIOUS...
WELL... THEY'LL GET TIRED...
THE FLYING BANDIT!
...EVENTUALLY!
THE FLYING BANDIT!

SEE, YOU WERE JUST BEING *SILLY* MAKING A BIG DEAL OUT OF THIS!

YES, YOU WERE RIGHT...

HOW GOULD WE HAF KNOWN?

YEAH, HE'S REALLY VEWY NICE! SLURP!

YUMM, AND THESE *RICE BALLS* ARE ABSHOLUTELY DELISHUS!

THEY WOULDN'T HAPPEN TO BE THE ONES WE SHTOLE FROM THE EMPEROR, AND SOMEONE SHTOLE FROM US JUST AFTER?

THEY TASTE THE SAME!

MAYBE! WHO KNOWS?

WE'RE HERE...

BUT BEFORE WE GO INTO OUR *SECRET BASE,* YOU NEED TO SWEAR TO *NEVER* REVEAL IT...

PLEASE, SIR!

WE'D NEVER BETRAY SOMEONE WHO SHARED HIS RICE BALLS WITH US IN OUR HOUR OF NEED!

GOOD. FOLLOW ME...

Krrriiii...mmm

OOOH! HOW *ELEGANT!*

YOU HAVE VERY GOOD *TASTE!*

WHY DID WE NEVER GET A *SECRET BASE* LIKE THIS?

MAYBE YOU COULD LEAVE THE EMPEROR AND HELP THE FLYING BANDIT?

OHH....REALLY? YOU THINK HE'D ACCEPT US?

MAYBE, IF YOU ASK *NICELY....*

WELL, WELL.... WHAT DO WE HAVE HERE?

YOU SURE HAVE *GUTS,* COMING HERE AFTER EVERYTHING YOU PUT US THROUGH! AND IN SUCH GOOD COMPANY, TO BOOT!

YOU WEREN'T EXPECTING ME TO ACT LIKE A *NICE* AND *POLITE* LITTLE GIRL WERE YOU, MISTER CAT?!

WHY NOT?!

BECAUSE.... THAT'S NOT WHO I AM! I'M NOT LIKE THAT!

HAHAHA! WELL ISN'T THAT A *SURPRISE*! I HADN'T EVEN NOTICED!

WHAT'S IT TO YOU, ANYWAY?

EXPLAIN IT TO HER, *RAMINAGROBIS!*

WHAT'S IT TO YOU, ANYWAY?!

THAT'S ENOUGH, YOU TWO!

PFF... *RAMINAGROBIS?* THAT'S YOUR NAME? THAT'S SILLY!

HM! FINE... THERE'S MORE IMPORTANT STUFF TO TALK ABOUT. THE *BUTTERFLY* THE EMPEROR IS LOOKING FOR...

BECAUSE WE HAVE VERY GOOD REASON TO THINK THAT THE EMPEROR WOULD USE THE *BUTTERFLY* TO *TAKE OVER THE WORLD*...

TAKE OVER THE WORLD? WITH A *BUTTERFLY?* THAT DOESN'T MAKE ANY SENSE!

THERE'S AN ANCIENT STORY...

MORE THAN TWO THOUSAND YEARS AGO, THERE LIVED A *SAGE* NAMED

ZHUANG ZI...

WHEN HE FELL ASLEEP IN THE SONG EMPEROR'S GARDENS, HE HAD A *DREAM*...

...HE DREAMED OF A *BUTTERFLY!*

BUT IN HIS DREAM, THE *BUTTERFLY* FELL ASLEEP, TOO, AND HAD ITS OWN DREAM...

THE BUTTERFLY DREAMED OF ZHUANG ZI SLEEPING IN THE EMPEROR'S GARDENS!

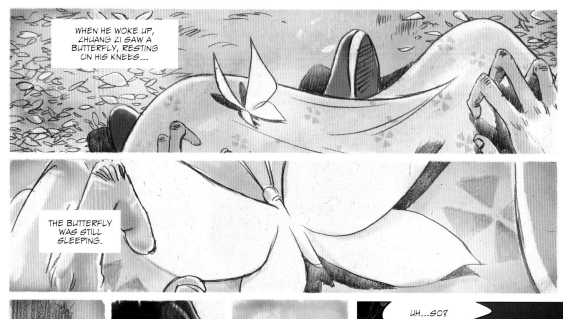

WHEN HE WOKE UP, ZHUANG ZI SAW A BUTTERFLY, RESTING ON HIS KNEES....

THE BUTTERFLY WAS STILL SLEEPING.

ZHUANG ZI WAS THEN SEIZED BY A SCARY THOUGHT....

WAS HE **REALLY** ZHUANG ZI, THE SAGE WHO HAD FALLEN ASLEEP IN THE EMPEROR'S GARDENS?

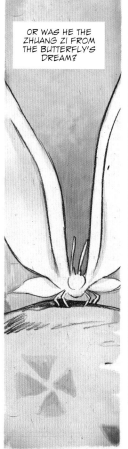

OR WAS HE THE ZHUANG ZI FROM THE BUTTERFLY'S DREAM?

UH....SO?

WELL, IT'S **OBVIOUS!**

?

OBVIOUS JUST TO CRAZY CATS, OR TO NORMAL PEOPLE LIKE US, TOO?

WE HAVE REASON TO BELIEVE THAT THE BUTTERFLY SEARCHING FOR THE EMPEROR IS THE *SAME ONE* THAT ZHUANG ZI DESCRIBED...

THAT'S NOT POSSIBLE! NO *BUTTERFLY* CAN *LIVE* THAT LONG!

IS IT TRUE? THEY CAN'T?

OH.... HOW SAD!

THIS ONE CAN...

BECAUSE IT'S THE *BUTTERFLY* THAT'S *DREAMING* OF THIS WORLD!

!!!

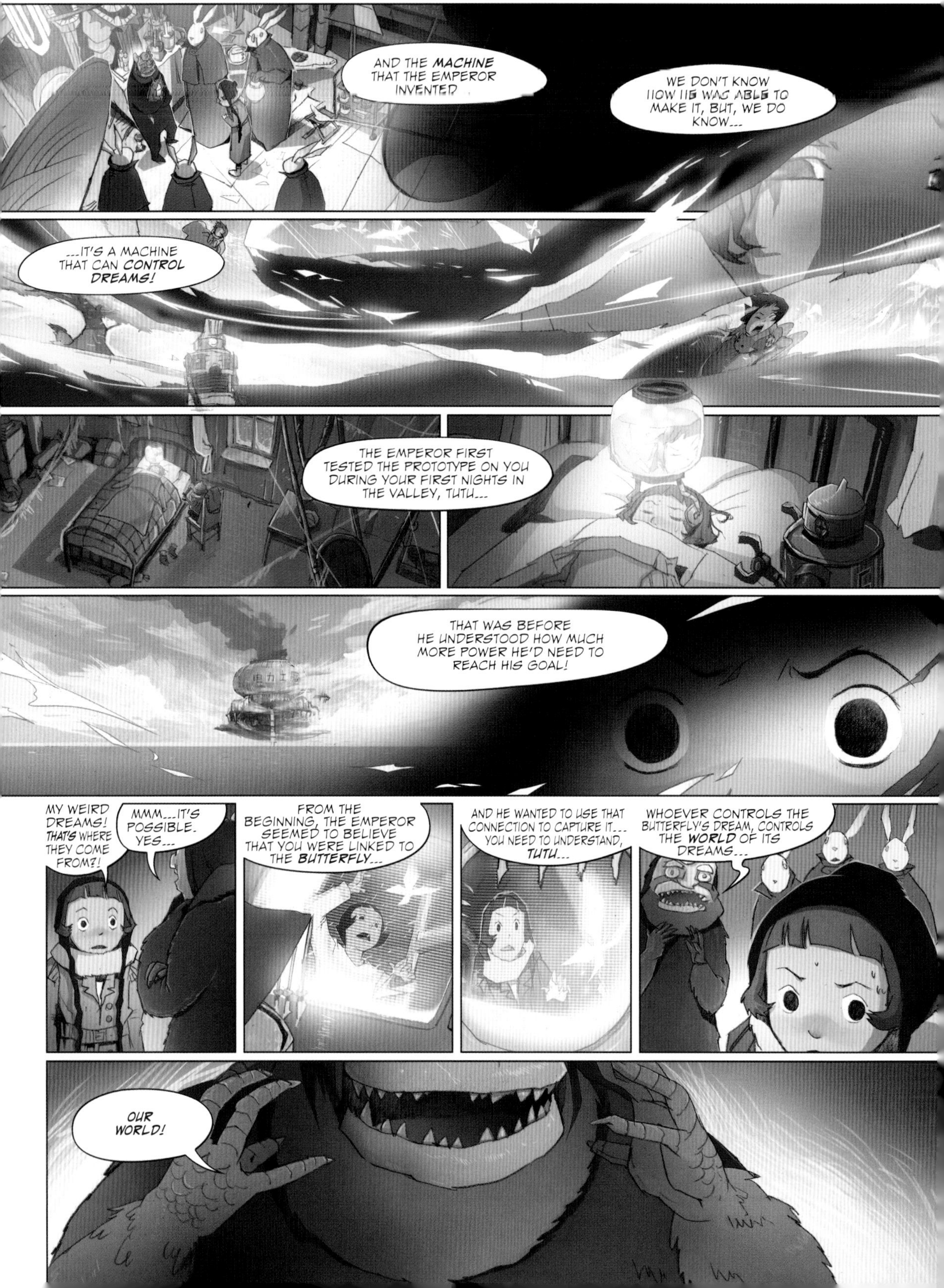
AND THE MACHINE THAT THE EMPEROR INVENTED
WE DON'T KNOW HOW HE WAS ABLE TO MAKE IT, BUT, WE DO KNOW...
...IT'S A MACHINE THAT CAN CONTROL DREAMS!
THE EMPEROR FIRST TESTED THE PROTOTYPE ON YOU DURING YOUR FIRST NIGHTS IN THE VALLEY, TUTU...
THAT WAS BEFORE HE UNDERSTOOD HOW MUCH MORE POWER HE'D NEED TO REACH HIS GOAL!
MY WEIRD DREAMS! THAT'S WHERE THEY COME FROM?!
MMM...IT'S POSSIBLE. YES...
FROM THE BEGINNING, THE EMPEROR SEEMED TO BELIEVE THAT YOU WERE LINKED TO THE BUTTERFLY...
AND HE WANTED TO USE THAT CONNECTION TO CAPTURE IT... YOU NEED TO UNDERSTAND, TUTU...
WHOEVER CONTROLS THE BUTTERFLY'S DREAM, CONTROLS THE WORLD OF ITS DREAMS...
OUR WORLD!

YOU COULD'VE AT LEAST TOLD ME A LITTLE EARLIER!

THAT'S WHAT WE'VE BEEN TRYING TO DO FROM THE *BEGINNING:* WARN YOU!

NO YOU HAVEN'T! YOU'VE BEEN KEEPING THINGS FROM ME THE WHOLE TIME!

NOT AT ALL!

YES, YOU HAVE!

?!

YOU HAVE AND YOU KNOW IT!

NO, WE WEREN'T AND I DON'T!

ENOUGH! THIS ISN'T THE TIME TO ARGUE!

IF WE DON'T ACT FAST, THE EMPEROR WILL PUT HIS *TERRIBLE PLAN* INTO ACTION!

DO YOU HAVE A PLAN?

I DON'T HAVE THE SLIGHTEST IDEA...

NOT THE SLIGHTEST IDEA? OH, BUT...

!!!

THE FLYING BANDIT CAN'T SAVE US!

WE'RE DOOMED!

THE EMPEROR WILL MESS WITH OUR *DREAMS* AND TICKLE OUR *NIGHTMARES!*

ARE YOU REALLY NOT GOING TO DO ANYTHING?

BUT TIME IS SHORT, AND I CAN'T DO IT ALONE. I NEED YOUR *HELP!*

I SAID I DIDN'T HAVE A PLAN, NOT THAT I WASN'T GOING TO *ACT...*

WE CAN HELP HIM! ISN'T THAT RIGHT?!

YES, MAYBE...

WILL IT BE DANGEROUS?!

WITHOUT A DOUBT! *DREAMS ARE FRAGILE.* THIS ONE MOST OF ALL!

UH...REALLY, REALLY DANGEROUS?

WE'D LIKE TO KNOW BEFOREHAND, IF THAT'S THE CASE....

AAAAH! I KNEW YOU WOULDN'T LET US DOWN! HOW BRAVE! HOW COURAGEOUS! COME HERE SO I CAN HUG YOU!

SAY...IF IT GETS REALLY DANGEROUS, COULD WE GET AN EXTRA SERVING OF RICE BALLS?

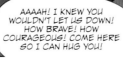

WELL, THIS IS NICE AND ALL....BUT WHAT ARE WE ACTUALLY DOING?

EVERYBODY GOES HOME UNTIL WE GET THE SIGNAL....

BUT....UH.... WHAT IF THE EMPEROR MANAGES TO UNDERSTAND THE **MYSTERY** OF THE BUTTERFLY'S DREAM BEFORE THE FLYING BANDIT'S SIGNAL?

THEN THIS VALLEY WILL BE FOREVER LOST TO HIS **ETERNAL WINTER**....

AND SOON, IT WOULD BE OUR DREAMS AND OUR LIVES THAT WOULD FALL UNDER HIS CONTROL....

BRRR.... THAT'S A **COLD** THOUGHT....

COLD AND SAD....

STUCK LIKE THIS, FOREVER?

SO...YOU THINK YOU'RE MORE **CLEVER** THAN EVERYONE ELSE, MISS TUTU?

YOU THINK THAT WITH A LITTLE ROCKET SCIENCE, YOU CAN **REBEL** WHENEVER YOU WANT...

YOU THINK I WAITED FOR THE **BUTTERFLY** BEFORE LEARNING ALL OF YOUR **DREAMS?**

MAYBE YOU'RE WAITING FOR SOME KIND OF MIRACLE? HAHAHA!

HAHAHA! PATHETIC!

AS IF THE ONLY CAPABLE MIND HERE (MINE!) COULDN'T STAND AGAINST YOUR PITIFUL **RESISTANCE...**

SO, LITTLE MISS **PEST...**

HA! HA! HA!

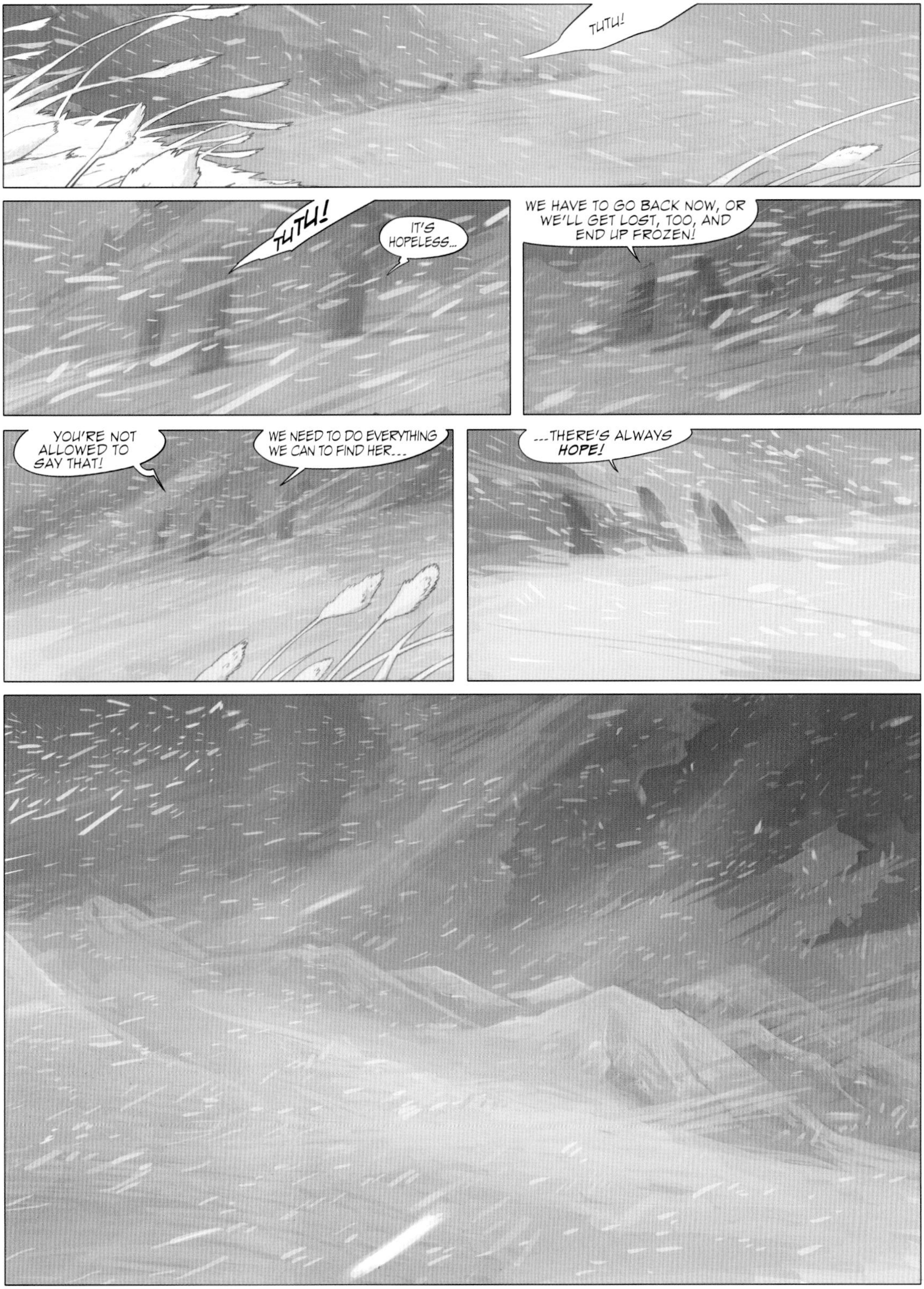
TUTU!
TUTU!
IT'S HOPELESS...
WE HAVE TO GO BACK NOW, OR WE'LL GET LOST, TOO, AND END UP FROZEN!
YOU'RE NOT ALLOWED TO SAY THAT!
WE NEED TO DO EVERYTHING WE CAN TO FIND HER...
...THERE'S ALWAYS HOPE!

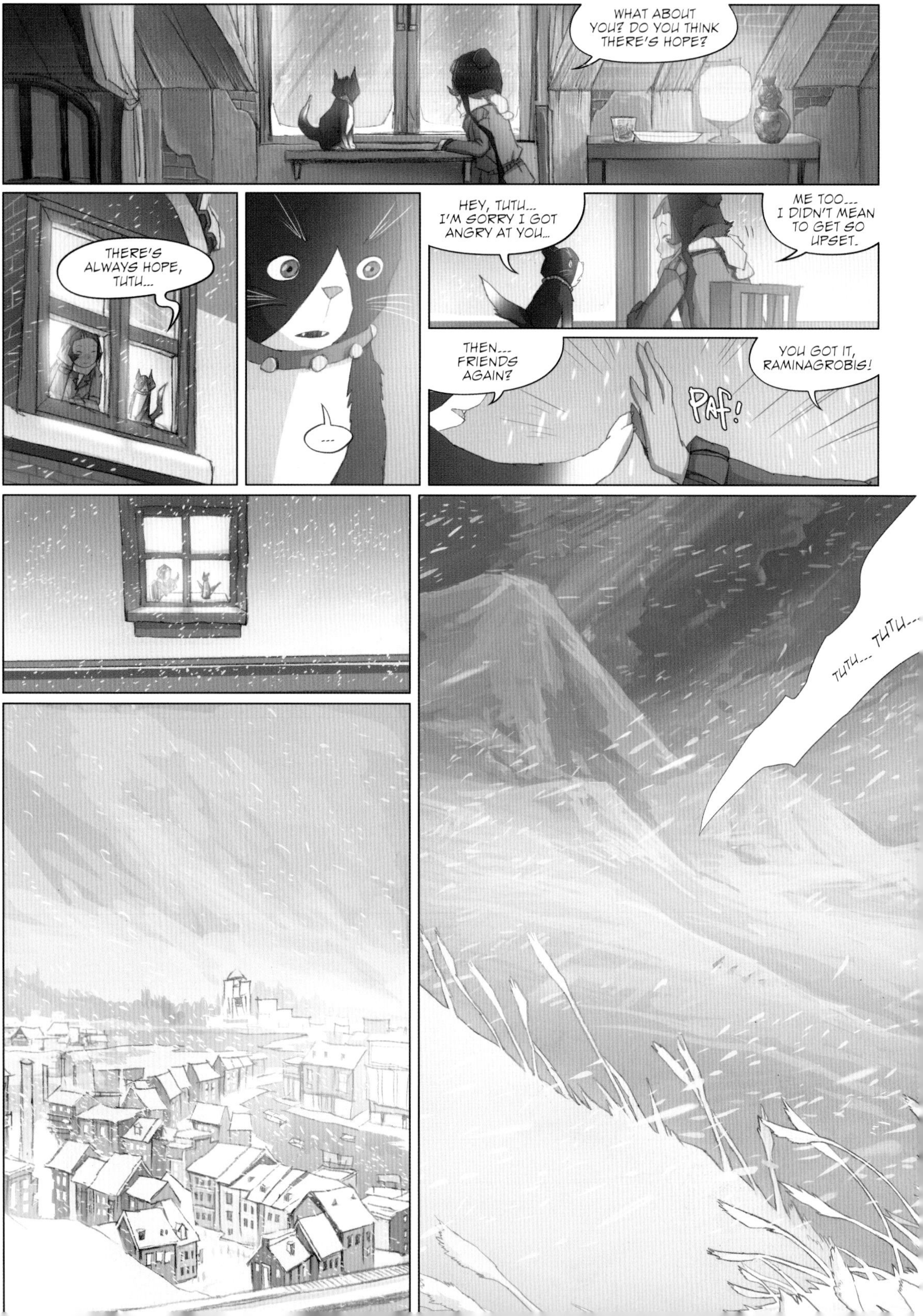
WHAT ABOUT YOU? DO YOU THINK THERE'S HOPE?
THERE'S ALWAYS HOPE, TUTU...
...
HEY, TUTU... I'M SORRY I GOT ANGRY AT YOU...
ME TOO... I DIDN'T MEAN TO GET SO UPSET.
THEN... FRIENDS AGAIN?
YOU GOT IT, RAMINAGROBIS!
PAF!
TUTU... TUTU...

WHAT A STRANGE DREAM...

IT'S THE **SAME** EVERY TIME...

BUT SOMEHOW SO **DIFFERENT!**

TUTU! IT'S USELESS TO WAIT ANY LONGER! HE WON'T BE COMING TODAY!

?!

OH! IT'S YOU? I WAS **SCARED** THAT YOU WERE THAT TERRIBLE **EMPEROR!**

THAT'S UP TO YOU. IT'S YOUR DREAM, AFTER ALL...

SO WE'RE **FRIENDS** AGAIN?

OBVIOUSLY!

EVEN IN MY **DREAM?**

WHY NOT?!

YAAAWN!

HUH?

THESE DREAMS ARE ALWAYS SO *DUMB*....BUT THERE WAS NO *BUTTERFLY* THIS TIME....

SO....WHAT NOW?

OH! YES, OF COURSE!

THAT'S WHAT I HAVE TO DO! I NEED TO ORGANIZE A *REVOLUTION!*

HOW DO PEOPLE ORGANIZE REVOLUTIONS USUALLY? WHO DO THEY SEND INVITES TO?

THEY DON'T TEACH THIS KIND OF THING IN SCHOOL...

HEY! I NEED HELP HERE...

DID YOU HEAR ME?

OH! HELLO...

SO, ARE YOU GOING TO HELP ME?

ME, HELP YOU? BUT I'M NOT SUPPOSED TO HELP YOU, I'M SUPPOSED TO SPY ON YOU!

I KNOW, BUT WHO ELSE IS THERE?

YOU DON'T KNOW THE EMPEROR. SOMEBODY COULD BE SPYING ON ME WHILE I SPY ON YOU...

REALLY?

REALLY!

YOU HAVE TO UNDERSTAND, FOR NOW, WE STILL NEED TO KEEP UP APPEARANCES....

AND HOW AM I GOING TO **SAVE** THAT BUTTERFLY WITH YOU **RABBIT SPIES** ALL PRETENDING....THAT'S NOT VERY PRACTICAL!

...

AND WHY IS THE EMPEROR LETTING ME WALK AROUND FREE AND....WATCHED...

I'M SUPPOSED TO BE A **TERRIBLE THREAT** TO HIM!

PFFF....HIM? YOU DON'T HAVE TO WORRY, HE THINKS HE'S ALREADY **WON!**

OH, REALLY?

WELL, YES.... OR ELSE HE WOULDN'T LET US **SPY** ON YOU OURSELVES.... WE'RE NOT VERY **CAPABLE**, YOU KNOW....

YOUR BUS IS HERE, MISS TUTU. PLEASE, BE **CAREFUL.**

THANK YOU, MISTER **TRASH RABBIT!**

SHHH! YOU'RE GOING TO GET US **CAUGHT!**

ALRIGHT, LET'S GO OVER THIS AGAIN... I NEED TO ORGANIZE A *REVOLUTION* TO DETHRONE THE EMPEROR, *FREE* THE BUTTERFLY THAT'S DREAMING UP THE ENTIRE WORLD, AND SAVE THE VALLEY FROM ITS *ETERNAL WINTER!*

I CAN COUNT ON HELP FROM THE FLYING BANDIT AND HIS *DUMB CAT*...

IF I COULD MAKE THEM UNDERSTAND THAT *KIDS* CAN BE SERIOUS, I COULD MAYBE ALSO GET HELP FROM THE *FACTORY WORKERS*...

THE KIDS! OF COURSE!

I NEED TO GET HELP FROM LAN AND HIS *REBELS!*

STOP THE BUS!

RIGHT NOW!

WHAT'S GOING ON?

AN EMERGENCY? A CATASTROPHE? A DISASTER?

THAT CHILD IS A REAL PEST!

SORRY, I GOT ON THE WRONG BUS...

NOW...
NOW...

WHERE COULD THEY BE? THEY ALWAYS CHANGE HIDING PLACES...

OH! I HAVE AN IDEA!

THEY'RE KIDS, RIGHT?

AND KIDS ARE THE SAME EVERYWHERE!

GIVE ME THREE BAGS OF CANDY, PLEASE! SWEET AND SOUR!

ONE LAST THING AND WE'RE READY...

LET'S JUST HOPE IT DOESN'T TAKE TOO LONG...

TOO LONG...

I'M SURE TO CATCH ONE OR TWO WITH THIS...

AH! GOT ONE!

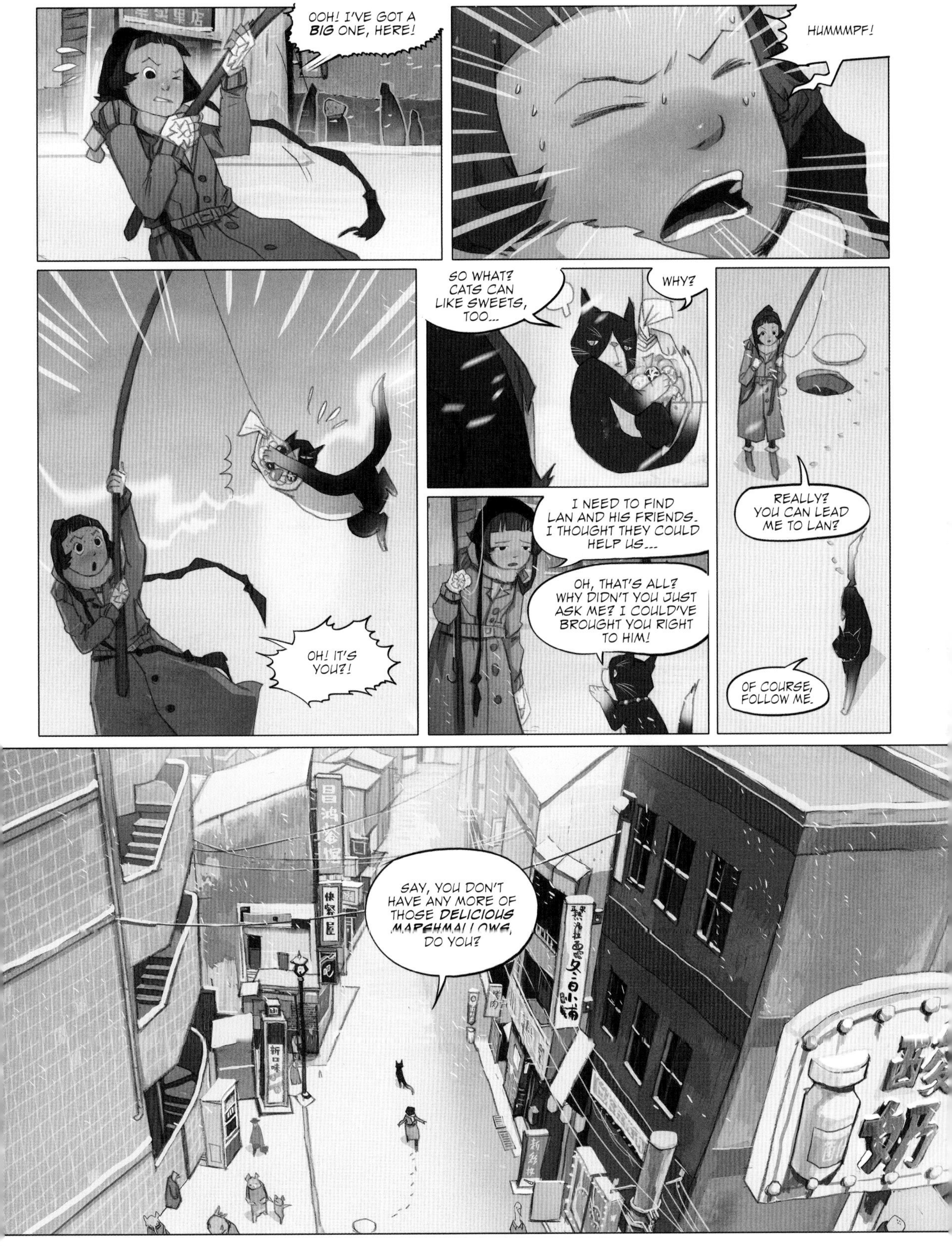

OOH! I'VE GOT A BIG ONE, HERE!
HUMMMPF!
OH! IT'S YOU?!
SO WHAT? CATS CAN LIKE SWEETS, TOO...
WHY?
I NEED TO FIND LAN AND HIS FRIENDS. I THOUGHT THEY COULD HELP US...
OH, THAT'S ALL? WHY DIDN'T YOU JUST ASK ME? I COULD'VE BROUGHT YOU RIGHT TO HIM!
REALLY? YOU CAN LEAD ME TO LAN?
OF COURSE, FOLLOW ME.
SAY, YOU DON'T HAVE ANY MORE OF THOSE DELICIOUS MARSHMALLOWS, DO YOU?

HAHAHA! THIS IS REALLY TOO *FUNNY!*

YES, *MASTER....*

THAT LITTLE *IDIOT* REALLY THINKS SHE CAN INSTIGATE A *REVOLUTION* HERE?! IN *MY* VALLEY?! ISN'T THAT RIDICULOUS?

COMPLETELY, MASTER....

EVER SINCE WE'VE BEEN TESTING OUR *MACHINE* ON THIS *BUTTERFLY*, THINGS HAVE BEEN CHANGING.... ITS POWER IS STILL LIMITED, BUT SOON IT WILL COME TO CONTROL THE WORLD *COMPLETELY....*

...IN FACT, I CAN'T HELP BUT FEEL THAT THE *BUTTERFLY* IS HAVING A DIFFICULT TIME *CONTROLLING* YOU. YOU'RE STILL SO STUBBORN....

GO HOME. I WOULDN'T WANT YOU TO RETURN TO YOUR SENSES IN *MY* PRESENCE. THAT WOULD BE A RATHER *UNFORTUNATE* EXPERIENCE....

AS YOU DESIRE, MASTER....

I'LL CALL FOR YOU AGAIN. SOON. WHEN I'LL HAVE *COMPLETELY* ASSERTED MY CONTROL....

YES, MASTER....

ARE YOU SURE THIS IS THE PLACE? IT DOESN'T LOOK LIKE THE SHOP YOU BROUGHT ME TO LAST TIME...

OPEN THE DOOR. YOU'LL SEE...

MAKE UP YOUR MIND! ARE YOU COMING OR GOING?

?!

UH, COMING, I GUESS....HOW DID YOU KNOW IT WAS ME?

BE QUIET AND LET US *WORK IN PEACE*, OR WE'LL NEVER MAKE IT!

WHAT? YOU'RE GOING TO BE THAT RUDE TO *ME?*

MMM....

PAF

♪♪

SBROAF

THERE, NOW IT'S *RUINED!* WE'LL HAVE TO START OVER FROM THE *BEGINNING!*

WE'LL NEVER MANAGE TO THREAD THIS LACE; IT'S TOO *STUBBORN!*

OH, IT'S YOU TUTU? TAKES GUTS TO SHOW UP LIKE THIS, AFTER ALL THIS *TIME!* I IMAGINE YOU WANT SOMETHING.

SO, WHAT DO YOU NEED?

I NEED YOUR HELP FOR A *REVOLUTION!*

A *REVOLUTION?* THAT'S ALL?

YES, ONE THAT'S NOT TOO BIG OR TOO SMALL. JUST THE *RIGHT* SIZE SO WE CAN GET RID OF THAT AWFUL *EMPEROR!*

MMM, I SEE...

AND WOULD YOU LIKE US TO DELIVER IT TO YOUR HOME, OR DO YOU WANT TO COME AND PICK IT UP WHEN IT'S READY?

OOOH! YOU *DELIVER?* THAT'S PERFECT! COULD YOU BRING IT TO ME IN TWO DAYS DURING *BREAKFAST?*

WE CAN'T START A *REVOLUTION* ON AN EMPTY STOMACH, RIGHT?

PFF....SORRY TUTU, BUT THERE'S NOTHING WE CAN DO FOR YOU...

AND WHY'S THAT? YOU SAID YOU COULD!

BUT AS SOON AS IT GETS *SERIOUS*, YOU AND YOUR FRIENDS JUST RUN AWAY!

OH NO, TUTU, YOU DON'T UNDERSTAND... EVEN IF YOU ARE AN *IMPULSIVE* GIRL WHO ONLY THINKS ABOUT HER OWN *PROBLEMS*...

WE CAN PARTICIPATE, BUT THERE'S ONE THING WE CAN'T DO FOR YOU...YOU NEED TO BELIEVE YOU'RE CAPABLE OF PULLING OFF THIS *REVOLUTION* BY YOURSELF! OTHERWISE IT WON'T WORK!

BY MYSELF? ARE YOU CRAZY? *NOBODY* CAN PULL OFF A REVOLUTION ALL ALONE!

AND HOW COULD I? I DON'T EVEN KNOW WHAT A REVOLUTION *LOOKS* LIKE!

YOU SEE? THAT'S WHAT I'M TALKING ABOUT!

IT'S SIMPLE! INSTEAD OF JUST *COMPLAINING* ALL THE TIME, YOU JUST NEED TO START TELLING YOURSELF THAT YOU CAN CHANGE THE WORLD AROUND YOU...

THAT'S WHAT THE *BUTTERFLY* DOES... ISN'T IT SUPPOSED TO *DREAM UP* THE WORLD?

SO YOU NEED TO BECOME LIKE THE *BUTTERFLY*...

BECOME LIKE THE **BUTTERFLY**... HE SURE THINKS HE'S FUNNY!

HOW DOES SOMEONE BECOME LIKE A BUTTERFLY AT ALL?

HOW CAN I DREAM UP AN **ENTIRE** WORLD....

HELP!

LAN?

WHY DID YOU **ABANDON** US WHEN WE NEEDED YOU MOST?

THAT'S NOT TRUE! I **STAYED!** I TRIED TO **HELP** YOU!

DON'T FORGET US, TUTU! PLEASE, YOU NEED TO REMEMBER US....ALWAYS!

LAN! NOOOO--

--OOOO!

WHAT DID HE MEAN? I HAVE TO *REMEMBER* HIM?

WHAT WOULD HAPPEN IF I FORGOT HIM? WOULD HE DISAPPEAR LIKE IN MY *DREAM?*

I DON'T HAVE THAT KIND OF POWER, DO I?

MMM...I GUESS IT WOULD MAKE THINGS EASIER...

MAYBE I SHOULD TRY ON THAT TRASH CAN...

GNNNN...

HMM...DOESN'T SEEM TO BE WORKING...

HARDER THEN! GNNNNN! COME ON, TRASH CAN, I ALREADY FORGOT ABOUT YOU, AND BY THE *POWER* OF MY *WAKING DREAM*, I WANT YOU TO DISAPPEAR!

ARE YOU CRAZY?! STOP! YOU'RE *SCARING* ME!

OH! YOU AGAIN? I THOUGHT I WAS GOING *CRAZY!*

YOU NEED TO STOP HIDING IN TRASH CANS LIKE THAT! IT'S NOT HYGIENIC!

I *PROMISE* I WON'T HIDE IN THEM ANYMORE! BUT PLEASE, DON'T MAKE ME *DISAPPEAR!*

MMM...IT DOESN'T SEEM TO BE WORKING, BUT THIS RABBIT SEEMS TO THINK I COULD....

THIS TIME, YOU'RE GOING TO TELL ME HOW I CAN START A *REVOLUTION!*

OF COURSE... UH....OR ELSE WHAT, AGAIN?

FINE...I'LL BE *GENEROUS.* I WON'T MAKE YOU DISAPPEAR *THIS* TIME... BUT YOU'LL HAVE TO DO SOMETHING FOR ME IN RETURN...

OH! YES, OF COURSE! ANYTHING YOU WANT....

OR ELSE ZAP! ZAP! ZAP! NO MORE *TRASH CAN* AND NO MORE *RABBIT!*

AAAAAH! NO, PLEASE! I BEG YOU! I'LL TELL YOU EVERYTHING!

WHY DON'T YOU GO SEE THE *ANIMALS* WHO WORK IN THE *FACTORY?*

THEY HAVE THE HARDEST LIVES OF ANYONE IN THE VALLEY.

AFTER *ME,* YOU MEAN?

OH! YES... AFTER *YOU,* OF COURSE.

PEOPLE ALWAYS FORGET HOW HARD LIFE IS FOR *LITTLE GIRLS* LIKE ME...

YES, IT'S OBVIOUS...

THANKS, *MISTER RABBIT!*

OH, THANK YOU! THANK YOU FOR YOUR *KINDNESS!* YOU'RE SO GOOD WITH ME! THANK YOU!

THANK YOU, THANK YOU, THANK YOU!

OK...THAT'S ENOUGH...

THAT'S ENOUGH... YOU CAN STOP NOW, YOU *BIG WEIRDO!*

IT WASN'T ENTIRELY UNAPPRECIATED, BUT STILL....

NOW, TO THE FACTORY!

ZAP! ZAP!

AAAHH! AAAAHHH!

ALWAYS THE SAME *CATCHPHRASE*...

AAAAH! THIS *GENTLE BREEZE* SMELLS LIKE FREEDOM...

HUH?! WHERE ARE ALL THE *WORKERS?*

WAIT FOR MY *SIGNAL!*

....NOW!

HEY! WHAT ARE YOU DOING?! IT'S ME! DON'T YOU REMEMBER?

LET'S BRING HER TO THE OTHERS, NOW...

DID WE HEAR CORRECTLY?

WHAT HAVE YOU HEARD?

THAT YOU'RE TRYING TO *ORGANIZE* A *REVOLUTION* IN OUR BEAUTIFUL VALLEY?

WHO ARE YOU? MORE OF THE EMPEROR'S *SPIES*? YOU DON'T *SCARE* ME!

YOU WILL BE SCARED...

UNLESS YOU TELL US EXACTLY WHAT YOU'RE *SCHEMING* AGAINST THE *EMPEROR!*

LAAAAAAN! HELP!

BUT...YOU KNOW LAN? YOU CAN UNTIE HER!

OF COURSE I KNOW HIM! WHAT DID YOU THINK?

WHAT? IT'S YOU? DID YOU TIE ME UP? I THOUGHT WE WERE *FRIENDS*...

WELL, TECHNICALLY YES...

WHAT ARE YOU SAYING? IT WAS *TECHNICALLY YOU*? OR *'TECHNICALLY' WE'RE FRIENDS!*

WELL...BOTH, I GUESS...

HM...I IMAGINE IT'S POSSIBLE...

BUT, IF I'M TECHNICALLY YOUR FRIEND, WHY DID YOU KIDNAP ME LIKE THIS?!

WELL, WE HEARD WHAT YOU WERE UP TO, AND IT SEEMED LIKE THE BEST WAY TO MAKE SURE YOU WERE BEING *SINCERE.*

IF WE WERE GOING TO HELP YOU, WE NEEDED TO BE *SURE* THAT WE CAN STAND BEHIND YOUR *CAUSE*. MAKES SENSE, DOESN'T IT?

SENSE? I'LL TELL YOU WHAT WOULD MAKE SENSE TO ME...

BECAUSE YOU'RE *FACTORY WORKERS*, AND THERE ARE *A LOT* OF YOU, AND YOU OCCUPY THE MOST *STRATEGIC* SPOT IN *THE VALLEY*... YOU COULD...

WE COULD?

YOU COULD POTENTIALLY...

YES! YOU COULD. I'M *SURE* OF IT!

COULD WHAT?!

ON THE DAY... THE HOUR! WE'LL COME UP WITH A *SIGNAL*...

TAKE THIS *FLYING LANTERN,* TUTU....

ON THE DAY, YOU CAN SEND US A SIGNAL....

BUT *BEWARE....* THERE ARE A FEW *RULES* YOU'LL HAVE TO *FOLLOW* IF YOU REALLY WANT OUR HELP....

FIRST, YOU'LL HAVE TO SEND THE SIGNAL BEFORE OUR NEXT PRODUCTION OF ENERGY....

OTHERWISE, THE LANTERN WILL BE LOST AMONG THE OTHERS....

BUT THAT'S NOT ALL!

WE'VE LEARNED THAT THE EMPEROR HAS PUT TOGETHER A DIABOLICAL MACHINE....FOR NOW, THE MACHINE ISN'T FULLY FUNCTIONAL, BECAUSE THERE ISN'T ENOUGH ENERGY AVAILABLE....

SO THE EMPEROR CAN ONLY DO SO MUCH....

BUT WITH THE NEXT PRODUCTION, HE'LL HAVE ALL THE POWER HE NEEDS AT HIS DISPOSAL TO MAKE FULL USE OF HIS TERRIBLE INVENTION....

YOU NEED TO ACT BEFORE IT'S TOO LATE, TUTU....

AND YOU ONLY HAVE A FEW DAYS....

WELL, I SEEM TO BE MAKING PROGRESS...

I'VE GOT THE FLYING BANDIT HELPING ME...LAN AND THE OTHER *REBEL CHILDREN*...

AND NOW, THE *WORKERS* FROM THE FACTORY...

BUT I DON'T THINK IT'S GOING TO BE THAT EASY...

AND NOW THAT I'M THINKING ABOUT IT... WHY DID I SCREAM LAN'S NAME EARLIER?

I DON'T SEE HIM FOR A LONG TIME, *MIRACULOUSLY* FIND HIM AGAIN, AND ALL OF A SUDDEN I CAN'T STOP THINKING ABOUT HIM...IT'S PRETTY WEIRD...

AND WHY DIDN'T I CALL FOR THE FLYING BANDIT INSTEAD?

DOES THAT MEAN I WOULD RATHER BE SAVED BY LAN?

AND WHY WOULD I WANT TO BE *SAVED* IF I'M COMPLETELY CAPABLE OF *SAVING* MYSELF!

HEY! WHAT'S GOING ON HERE?!

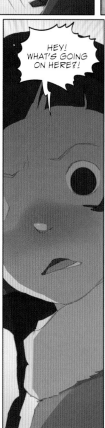

WHERE IS THIS BUS GOING?! *STOP!* I WANT TO GET OFF!

OH, COME ON! NOT AGAIN! WHAT DO YOU WANT WITH ME NOW?!

WE'RE REALLY SORRY ABOUT THIS, MISS TUTU, BUT NOW WE HAVE TO *TORTURE* YOU...

TORTURE ME? WHY? IT'S NOT *FAIR!*

BECAUSE WE HAVE TO STAY *LOYAL* TO THE EMPEROR, AND HE NEEDS SOME INFORMATION ABOUT YOUR LITTLE *REVOLUTION...*

SO YOU'RE GOING TO USE *DENTIST* TOOLS TO TORTURE ME?

YEAH, RIGHT!

OH NO! *DON'T WORRY!* WE HAVE SOMETHING MUCH MORE *TERRIBLE* IN STORE FOR YOU. YOU'RE GOING TO TELL US *EVERYTHING...*

OH NO, IT'S NOT THAT... BUT YOU'RE *RABBITS...*

YOU DON'T REALLY EXPECT ME TO BE *SCARED* OF GETTING TORTURED BY *RABBITS*, DO YOU?

WE'LL SEE!

Sdock

WHAT'S WRONG? AREN'T YOU *SCARED?*

LET'S SEE IF YOU CAN RESIST *THIS!*

OH MY GOD! WHAT IS THAT?!

A GOOSE FEATHER! OF THE UTMOST QUALITY! AS *SOFT* AS THEY COME!

TAKE OFF HER SHOES! WE'RE GOING TO GET STARTED!

ARE YOU SURE YOU DON'T WANT TO GIVE IT UP NOW? WE DON'T WANT TO DO THIS THE *HARD WAY...*

ESPECIALLY NOT WITH YOU!

FINE! YOU ASKED FOR IT!

AH! AH! AH! AH! STOP! *STOP!*

NO, NO, THAT'S ALRIGHT...DO YOUR JOBS, YOU MISERABLE *TRAITORS...*

STOP! I CAN'T TAKE ANY *MORE!*

HA! HA!

HA! HA!

HA! HA!

IT'S INHUMANE!

HA! HA! HA!

OH! LOOK WHAT YOU DID TO THESE *POOR RABBITS.* IT'S ALL YOUR FAULT!

KEEP TALKING, OR I'LL CONTINUE TO *TICKLE* YOUR FEET UNTIL THEY ALL *DIE* FROM *LAUGHTER...*

...LET THAT WEIGH ON YOUR *CONSCIENCE!*

OH NO! IT'S NOT *FAIR!* DON'T TRY AND *GUILT* ME! YOU'RE *RESPONSIBLE* FOR ALL THIS!

NO! NOT ME!

YES, YOU!

NO! NO! NO!

YES! YES! YES!

AHH-CHOO
AHH-CHOO
AAAAHH-CHOO

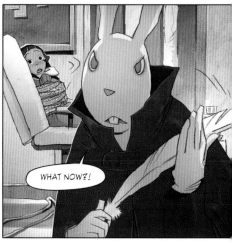

WHAT NOW?!

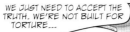

It's that **feather**. We're **allergic** to it!

=AHH—CHOO= =AHH—CHOO= **HELP!** I can't **BREATHE!**

We just need to accept the truth. We're not built for torture...

Even though we tried our best...we just can't do it...

Hey...Don't be so hard on yourselves. After all, it's not **YOUR** fault, it's just **ATAVISM**...

What? Did she say **ATAVISM**?

What is that? Is it a vegetable?

Something we **ATE**, but can't digest well?

Like **BEETS**, for example?

Are you sure that she didn't say **ASPARAGUS**?

No, **ATAVISM**! It's your tendencies as **KIND RABBITS** instead of **TORTURERS**!

Oh? So the **BEETS** make it impossible for us to **TORTURE** people?

No **STUPID**, you don't get it! It's **ASPARAGUS**!

WE'RE REALLY *TERRIBLE SPIES*...WHAT'S GOING TO HAPPEN TO US?

MAYBE YOU COULD HELP WITH MY *REVOLUTION?*

YOU THINK SO? REALLY?

OH NO, THAT'S TOO MUCH! WE CAN'T ACCEPT!

NO, YOU CAN... COME BACK! THE *CRAZIER* WE GET, THE MORE *RICE BALLS* WE'LL HAVE!

WELL, IF IT'S A *FRIENDLY INVITATION*, WE CAN'T VERY WELL REFUSE.

LET'S REJOIN THE REVOLUTION!

REVOLUTION!

WHAT A DAY!

I'M EXHAUSTED!

I STILL HAVE TO HIDE THAT *LANTERN* BEFORE I GO TO SLEEP....

IT SHOULD BE FINE UNDER MY BED... HEY?! WHAT....

OH! I COMPLETELY *FORGOT* ABOUT THIS!

A LITTLE READING BEFORE BED WON'T HURT....

NOW, WHERE WAS I....

DO YOU THINK SHE'LL BE ABLE TO SEE THIS *THROUGH*?

AFTER ALL, SHE'S JUST A *LITTLE GIRL*...

EXACTLY! LITTLE GIRLS ARE TOUGH...

SHE'S FULL OF *SURPRISES,* ISN'T SHE?

AND SHE'S TOUGHER THAN *ALL* OF THEM!

SHE'LL HAVE TO BE...

...SHE HAS A *DIFFICULT TRIAL* AHEAD!

THIS DREAM AGAIN....

?!

BUT IT'S....IT'S STILL *WINTER*....MAYBE.... MAYBE THIS ISN'T A *DREAM!*

WHO BROUGHT ME HERE?!

OH NO!

THE FLYING LANTERNS!

THEY'RE STARTING TO PRODUCE MORE ENERGY FOR THE EMPEROR'S PALACE! ALREADY!

IT'S ALL MY FAULT. THIS VALLEY WILL **NEVER** BE FREE....

I FAILED....

YOU'RE RIGHT. YOU'VE **LOST**, YOU FOOLISH GIRL....

YOUR REVOLUTION FAILED....

THE **DREAM OF THE BUTTERFLY** IS UNDER MY CONTROL....

WHO'S SAYING THAT? WHO ARE YOU?

WHAT, YOU DON'T RECOGNIZE ME?

I AM YOUR **EMPEROR** AND YOUR **MASTER**...

...**NOW** AND FOREVER!

AAAAAAAH!

OF COURSE! HOW DIDN'T I SEE THIS EARLIER? IT'S ALL JUST AN *ILLUSION!*

THERE'S NOT A MINUTE TO LOSE, THEN!

HE SURE *FOOLED* US WITH ALL HIS *ROBOTS!* BUT NOW HE'S ALL ALONE!

MISTER *COCKROACH,* YOUR HOUR IS *UP!*

TUTU? WHERE ARE YOU GOING LIKE THAT?

SORRY! I DON'T HAVE TIME TO EXPLAIN! I'M *LATE!*

THE *REVOLUTION* WAITS FOR NO ONE! QUICK! QUICK! QUICK!

QUICK! QUICK! QUICK!

HOW DOES THIS THING EVEN *WORK?!*

OH! I SEE!

PULL HERE!

LET'S PULL, THEN!

SO, WHAT NOW?

YES! IT'S WORKING!

YES! YES! YES!

NOW WE CAN GET THIS THING *STARTED!*

A *LANTERN?* BUT THERE'S NO PRODUCTION SCHEDULED FOR TODAY? WHERE DID IT COME FROM?

OH GOODNESS, YOU DON'T THINK IT'S THE *SIGNAL* THAT EVERYONE'S BEEN TALKING ABOUT!

YOU THINK SO?

THE *SIGNAL!* IT'S THE SIGNAL!

BY THE EMPEROR'S HOLY *KNEECAPS!* WHAT'S GOING TO HAPPEN?

QUICK! QUICK! COME OUTSIDE!

WHAT? WHAT'S GOING ON?

IS IT HER?

SHE ACTUALLY DID IT?

LAN! WHERE'S LAN?! GO FIND HIM! HE HAS TO SEE THIS!

SHE ACTUALLY DID IT! SHE SENT THE *SIGNAL!*

SO, WHAT DO YOU THINK?

WE WERE *RIGHT* TO *TRUST* HER...

WHAT NOW?

WE HELP HER, OF COURSE...

WHAT ELSE WOULD WE DO?

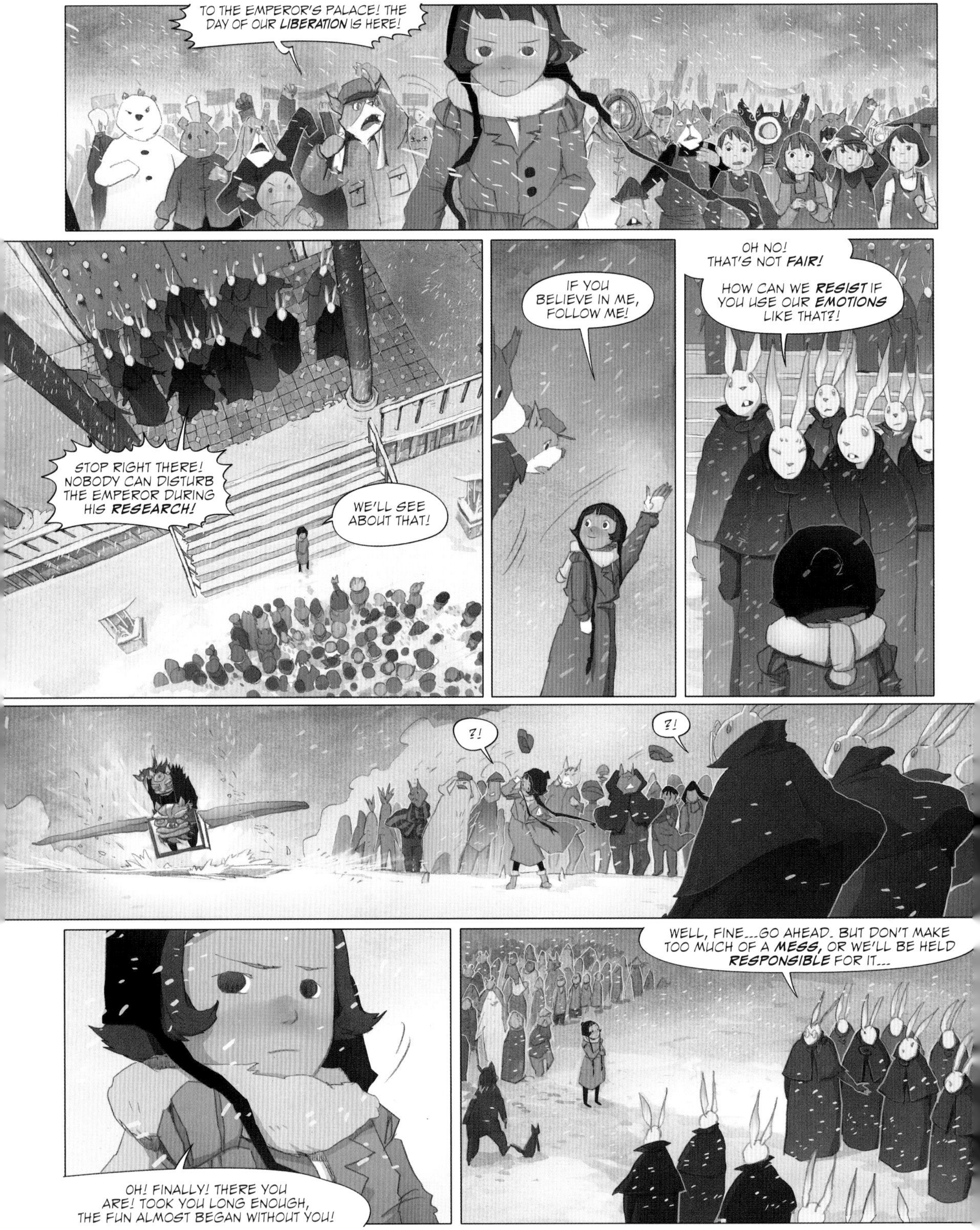
TO THE EMPEROR'S PALACE! THE DAY OF OUR LIBERATION IS HERE!
STOP RIGHT THERE! NOBODY CAN DISTURB THE EMPEROR DURING HIS RESEARCH!
WE'LL SEE ABOUT THAT!
IF YOU BELIEVE IN ME, FOLLOW ME!
OH NO! THAT'S NOT FAIR!
HOW CAN WE RESIST IF YOU USE OUR EMOTIONS LIKE THAT?!
?!
?!
OH! FINALLY! THERE YOU ARE! TOOK YOU LONG ENOUGH, THE FUN ALMOST BEGAN WITHOUT YOU!
WELL, FINE...GO AHEAD. BUT DON'T MAKE TOO MUCH OF A MESS, OR WE'LL BE HELD RESPONSIBLE FOR IT...

A FEW MORE ADJUSTMENTS AND YOUR **DREAMS** WILL BE **MINE**...

YOUR **MAJESTY!** THAT **ABOMINABLE LITTLE GIRL** HAS STARTED A **REVOLUTION!** SHE HAS A WHOLE CROWD WITH HER OUTSIDE!

I ALREADY PREDICTED HER DESPERATE EFFORTS AND UNDERMINING OF MY **SECRET POLICE!** IT MATTERS NOT!

MY **ARMY OF ROBOTS** WILL HOLD THEM BACK FOR A LITTLE WHILE...

SOON, WE'LL HAVE ALL THE ENERGY NECESSARY TO DASH ALL THEIR **HOPES** AND **DREAMS!**

GO, MY **CREATIONS!** GO AND TAKE CARE OF THEM ALL!

SOON, THEY'LL SEE THAT THEIR **FUTURE** BELONGS TO **US!**

RUN, MISS TUTU! WE WON'T BE ABLE TO HOLD THEM BACK FOR MUCH LONGER!

OH! YOU POOR LITTLE RABBITS!

THIS ISN'T A JOKE, TUTU! IF WE DON'T FIND A WAY TO SHUT DOWN THESE ROBOTS, WE'RE DONE FOR!

DON'T WORRY, I TOOK CARE OF IT! AT LEAST, I THINK I TOOK CARE OF IT....

THE SIGNAL! SHE SENT THE SIGNAL!

MMM....

MY FRIENDS, I THINK OUR LUNCH BREAK IS OVER....IT'S TIME WE GET BACK TO WORK.

WHAT? WHAT'S GOING ON?

WHY DO SUCH *IMBECILES* ALWAYS HAVE TO GET IN THE WAY OF MY *PLANS?!*

OH, GRAND EMPEROR, WE'LL SOON RUN OUT OF *ENERGY.* IF WE CAN'T RECHARGE, WE WON'T BE ABLE TO *DEFEND* THE *PALACE!*

AH! THOSE *MISERABLE WORKERS!* WHY DO THEY HAVE TO FIGHT AGAINST THEIR *MASTER?!*

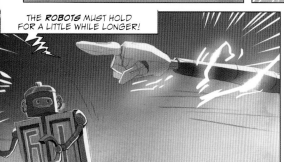

THE *ROBOTS* MUST HOLD FOR A LITTLE WHILE LONGER!

WHY DOES *NOBODY* EVER SEE THINGS *MY* WAY?!

IT'S NOT *FAIR!*

MISS TUTU, WE'RE *SORRY*, BUT WE CAN'T DO THIS MUCH LONGER!

WELL, AT LEAST WE *TRIED*...

I'M SO TIRED ANYWAYS...

TUTU, NO! YOU NEED TO GET *UP.* EVERYONE'S WATCHING YOU!

WHAT GOOD WILL IT DO NOW? I *FAILED.* I'LL NEVER BE ANYTHING BUT AN IMPULSIVE LITTLE GIRL.

OH NO, MISS TUTU! PLEASE! DON'T LET US DOWN!

WE'RE DOOMED!

WHAT WAS
THAT?!

SHTONK

IT'S A *MIRACLE!*

SHE CAN MAKE
MIRACLES, TOO!

SHE STRUCK DOWN THE
EMPEROR'S ROBOTS
WITH JUST A LOOK!

UM, WELL, I....

A *PROMISE*
IS A PROMISE!

HOORAY! THE
WAY IS CLEAR!

THERE HE IS!

?!

WHY IS THAT ONE STILL WORKING?

BAH! HE PROBABLY MADE SURE TO HAVE *EXTRA BATTERIES!* HE'S NOT THE *IMPERIAL ROBOT* FOR NOTHING!

IT'S OVER FOR YOU! LET THE BUTTERFLY GO!

NO....YOU CAN'T! YOU DON'T HAVE THE RIGHT! I AM YOUR *EMPEROR!*

NO! IT'S NOT OVER YET! FOLLOW ME!

?!

THE EMPEROR IS DEAD! *FREEDOM IS OURS!*

HE ESCAPED THROUGH HERE...

WHAT ARE YOU LOOKING FOR?

SHHH...

HERE WE ARE...

YOU'RE IN FOR A *BIG SURPRISE!*

?!

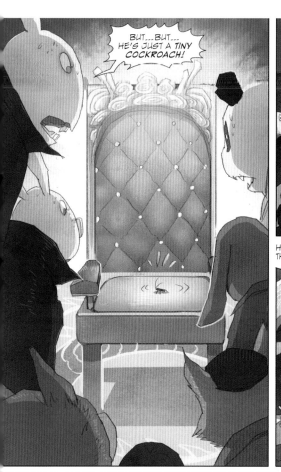

BUT...BUT... HE'S JUST A *TINY* COCKROACH!

HOW IS THIS POSSIBLE?!

HOW DID HE *TRICK* US FOR SO LONG?

WE LET OURSELVES BE MANIPULATED BY A PUPPET, WHEN FREEDOM WAS JUST A STEP AWAY!

HOW DID YOU UNCOVER THE *TRUTH*, MISS TUTU?

I DON'T KNOW, MAYBE I'M JUST THAT *CLEVER*...

SOMEONE'S FULL OF THEM- SELVES...

OKAY, WELL...

DO YOU REMEMBER THAT NIGHT IN THE LIBRARY?

AH! LET'S NOT TALK ABOUT THAT. WE WERE ALL SO *FRIGHTENED*...

WELL, I STOLE ONE OF THE BOOKS...

AH! DON'T TALK ABOUT THAT; I NEVER EVEN MANAGED TO GET MY PAWS ON IT...

THAT BOOK WAS WRITTEN BY THE EMPEROR HIMSELF, BEFORE HIS RISE TO POWER. IT EXPLAINED EVERYTHING....

IT WAS THE STORY OF A *LITTLE COCKROACH* HATED BY EVERYONE. FORCED TO *HIDE* IN THE SEWERS TO SURVIVE....

IT TOLD OF HIS GROWING RESENTMENT AND DESIRE FOR *VENGEANCE*....

ONE DAY, EVERYTHING WILL BE *MINE*!

HOW HE READ ABOUT THE STORY OF THE *DREAM OF THE BUTTERFLY*....

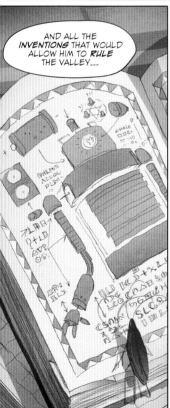

AND ALL THE *INVENTIONS* THAT WOULD ALLOW HIM TO *RULE* THE VALLEY....

IN ORDER TO TRAP IT IN AN *ETERNAL WINTER*.

BUT MAYBE HE WAS *WRONG* ABOUT *ONE* THING....

MAYBE THE *DREAM OF THE BUTTERFLY* WAS JUST A STORY ALL ALONG!

HOW UNEXPECTED...

WHAT ARE WE GOING TO DO WITH HIM NOW?

WE SHOULD MAKE HIM WORK IN THE *FACTORY* UNTIL THE END OF HIS DAYS!

SO HE CAN CONTINUE TO *POLLUTE* OUR *ATMOSPHERE*?! NO THANKS!

MAYBE WE SHOULD--

WATCH OUT! HE'S GETTING AWAY!

WHATEVER HAPPENS, HE CAN'T BE ALLOWED TO LEAVE THIS ROOM!

SGRATCH!

OOPS. SORRY....I THINK I MIGHT'VE JUST *STEPPED* ON HIM.

BLEH. WELL, I SUPPOSE WE'LL NEVER SEE THAT *EVIL EMPEROR* AGAIN.

SAY, YOU DIDN'T DO THAT ON *PURPOSE* DID YOU?

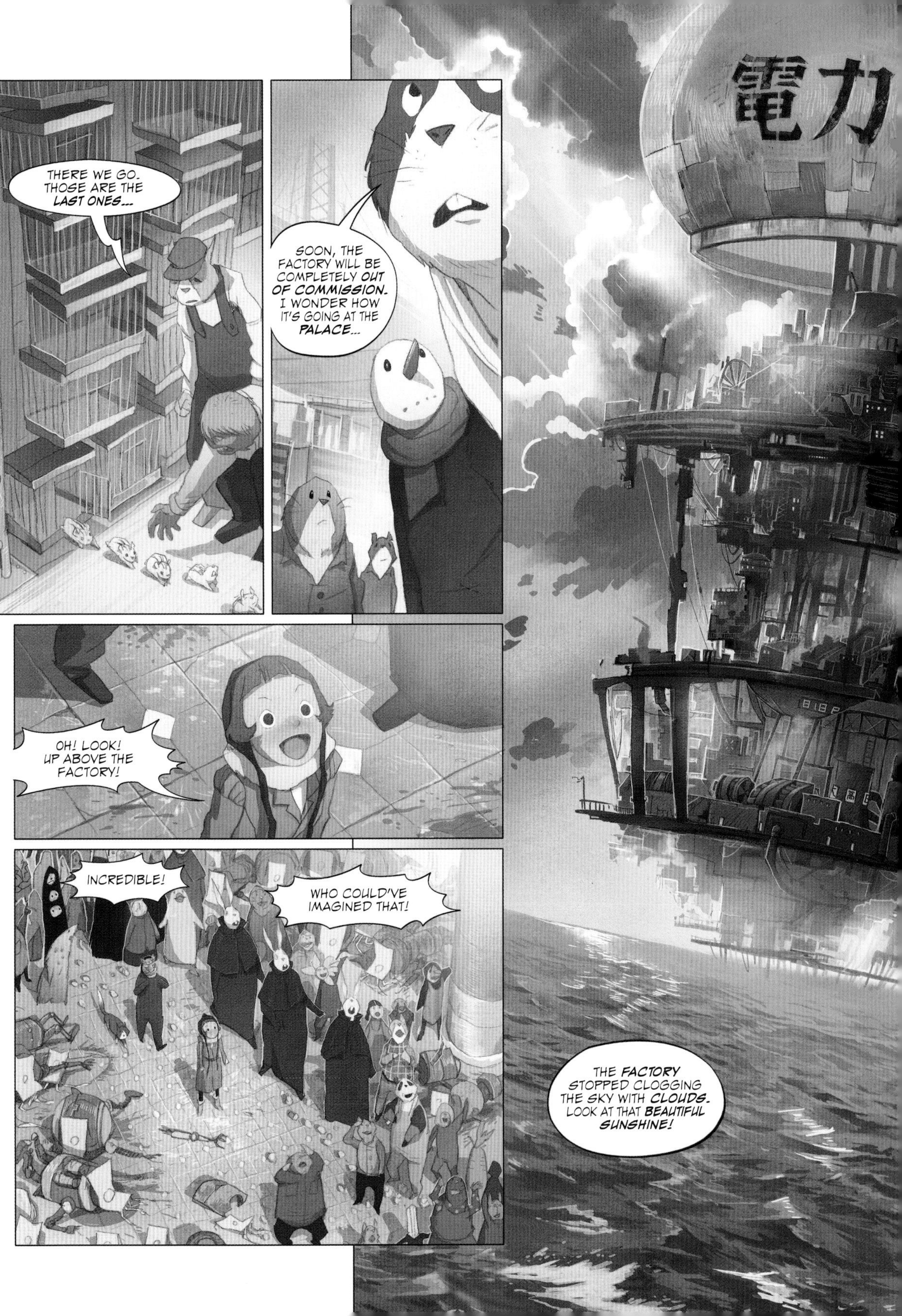

THERE WE GO. THOSE ARE THE LAST ONES...
SOON, THE FACTORY WILL BE COMPLETELY OUT OF COMMISSION. I WONDER HOW IT'S GOING AT THE PALACE...
電力
OH! LOOK! UP ABOVE THE FACTORY!
INCREDIBLE!
WHO COULD'VE IMAGINED THAT!
THE FACTORY STOPPED CLOGGING THE SKY WITH CLOUDS. LOOK AT THAT BEAUTIFUL SUNSHINE!

IT'S SO *HOT* ALL OF A SUDDEN!

YEAH, WHAT'S HAPPENING?

THE SKY! ALL THAT *LIGHT!*

IT LOOKS LIKE *WINTER* IS FINALLY *OVER!*

LOOK HOW HAPPY THEY ARE...

I'M SO GLAD!

IT'S LIKE THE END OF A *TERRIBLE* NIGHTMARE!

LOOK, MISS TUTU, EVEN YOUR HOST MOTHER...

FLYING IS SO *FREEING!* WE CAN FINALLY FLY AGAIN WITHOUT WORRYING ABOUT OUR WINGS FREEZING!

OOOOH!

CRASSH

OUCH!

MAYBE AFTER SOME *TRAINING...* IT REALLY WAS QUITE THE *LONG WINTER,* YOU KNOW....

LOOK AT THE CHERRY BLOSSOM TREE! IT'S INCREDIBLE!

IT'S ALREADY *BLOOMING!*

NATURE QUICKLY RECLAIMS ITS *PLACE...*

AND THESE *BUTTERFLIES!* THERE'RE THOUSANDS OF THEM!

I WONDER WHICH OF THEM IS *DREAMING UP A WORLD* RIGHT NOW...

IF ANY OF THEM ARE...

OH! BUT THERE IS ONE...

OH! NOW YOU DECIDE TO TALK? YOU HAVEN'T SAID A **WORD** SINCE WE'VE **FREED** THE VALLEY

THERE WASN'T AS MUCH TO SAY...

...AS THERE WAS TO BE THANKFUL FOR.

THERE IS A **BUTTERFLY** DREAMING UP OUR WORLD... BUT NO MATTER WHICH ONE IT IS, AS LONG AS IT CONTINUES TO **DREAM**...

BUT YOU'RE WRONG, TUTU. THE EMPEROR WAS RIGHT...

WHAT?!

THEN OUR WORLD MIGHT AS WELL BE YOUR **DAYDREAM** AFTER ALL.

FOR US, TODAY, **YOU ARE THE BUTTERFLY.**

THANK YOU FOR **FREEING** US, TUTU!

LAN?! IT WAS YOU? *THE WHOLE TIME?* WHY DIDN'T YOU SAY ANYTHING?!

I COULDN'T! I COULDN'T *INTERFERE* WITH YOUR *DREAM...*

BUT IF YOU DECIDED TO STAY WITH US, WE COULD....

BUT, I CAN'T, LAN! I HAVE TO GO HOME. YOU KNOW THAT....

THE *SNOW* THAT KEPT THIS VALLEY ISOLATED IS *MELTING.* THERE'S NOTHING *KEEPING* ME FROM GOING BACK NOW...

AND I'M SURE THEY'RE WAITING FOR ME ON THE OTHER SIDE...

YOU'RE RIGHT, TUTU. YOU'RE THE ONLY ONE WHO CAN MAKE THIS DECISION...

BUT I'LL COME BACK TO SEE YOU SOMEDAY...

GOODBYE, TUTU... DON'T FORGET US...

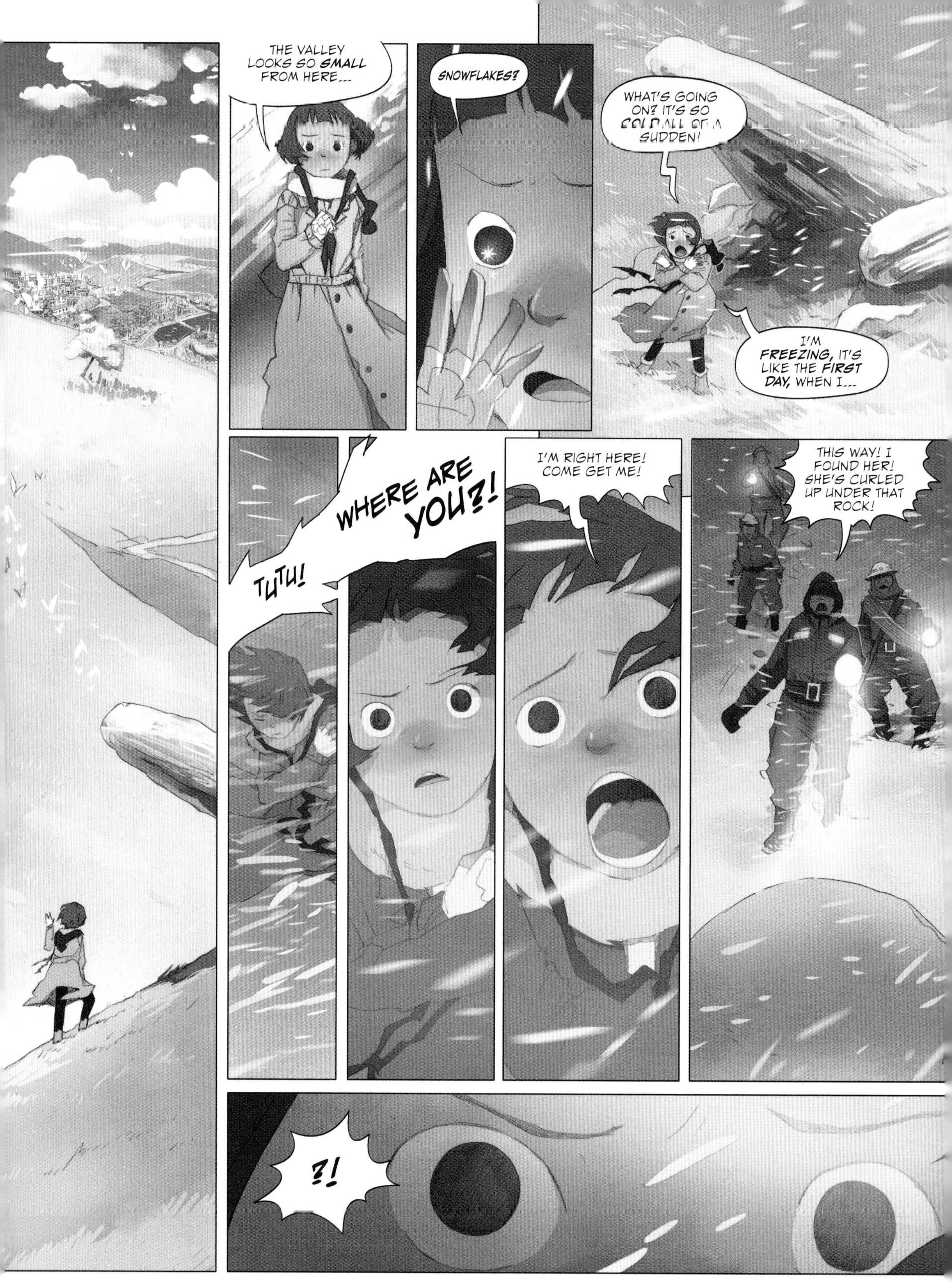
THE VALLEY LOOKS SO SMALL FROM HERE...
SNOWFLAKES?
WHAT'S GOING ON? IT'S SO COLD ALL OF A SUDDEN!
I'M FREEZING, IT'S LIKE THE FIRST DAY, WHEN I...
TUTU!
WHERE ARE YOU?!
I'M RIGHT HERE! COME GET ME!
THIS WAY! I FOUND HER! SHE'S CURLED UP UNDER THAT ROCK!
?!

OH NO! WE'RE *TOO LATE!* LOOK!

SHE PROBABLY USED THE ENTIRE BOX OF MATCHES TO WARM UP....

BUT IT WAS HOPELESS....

BUT I'M RIGHT HERE! CAN'T YOU HEAR ME?!

YOUR TURN, BOYS. NO NEED FOR US TO STICK AROUND ANY LONGER....

...YOU WERE RIGHT, LAN. IT'S MY DECISION TO MAKE....

WELL, SHE SURE *DUMPED* US...

...EVEN AFTER EVERYTHING WE *DID* FOR HER!

THAT'S ALWAYS HOW DREAMS *END*...WITHOUT ANY WARNING.

AND LOOK AT THEM! THEY'RE COMPLETELY *HEARTBROKEN!*

NO, YOU LOOK!

I'D RATHER NOT. IT *BUGS* ME, AND I'VE HAD MY FILL OF *BUGS*...

OVER THERE! BEHIND THE CHERRY BLOSSOMS!

IT'S JUST THE *FLOWERS* PLAYING *TRICKS* WITH YOUR *IMAGINATION*...

DON'T GET YOUR HOPES UP, LAN! IT'S AN *ILLUSION!*

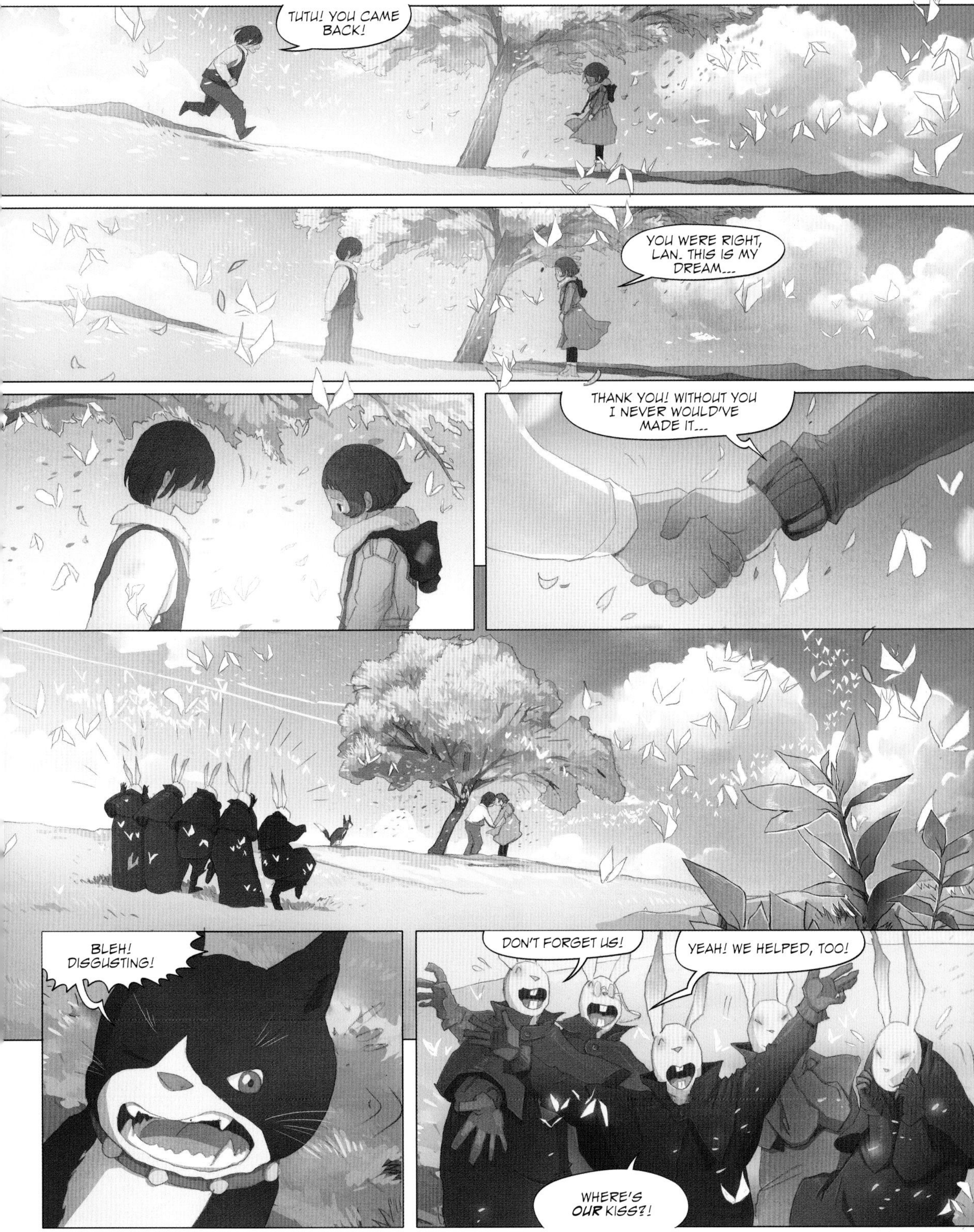
TUTU! YOU CAME BACK!
YOU WERE RIGHT, LAN. THIS IS MY DREAM...
THANK YOU! WITHOUT YOU I NEVER WOULD'VE MADE IT...
BLEH! DISGUSTING!
DON'T FORGET US!
YEAH! WE HELPED, TOO!
WHERE'S OUR KISS?!

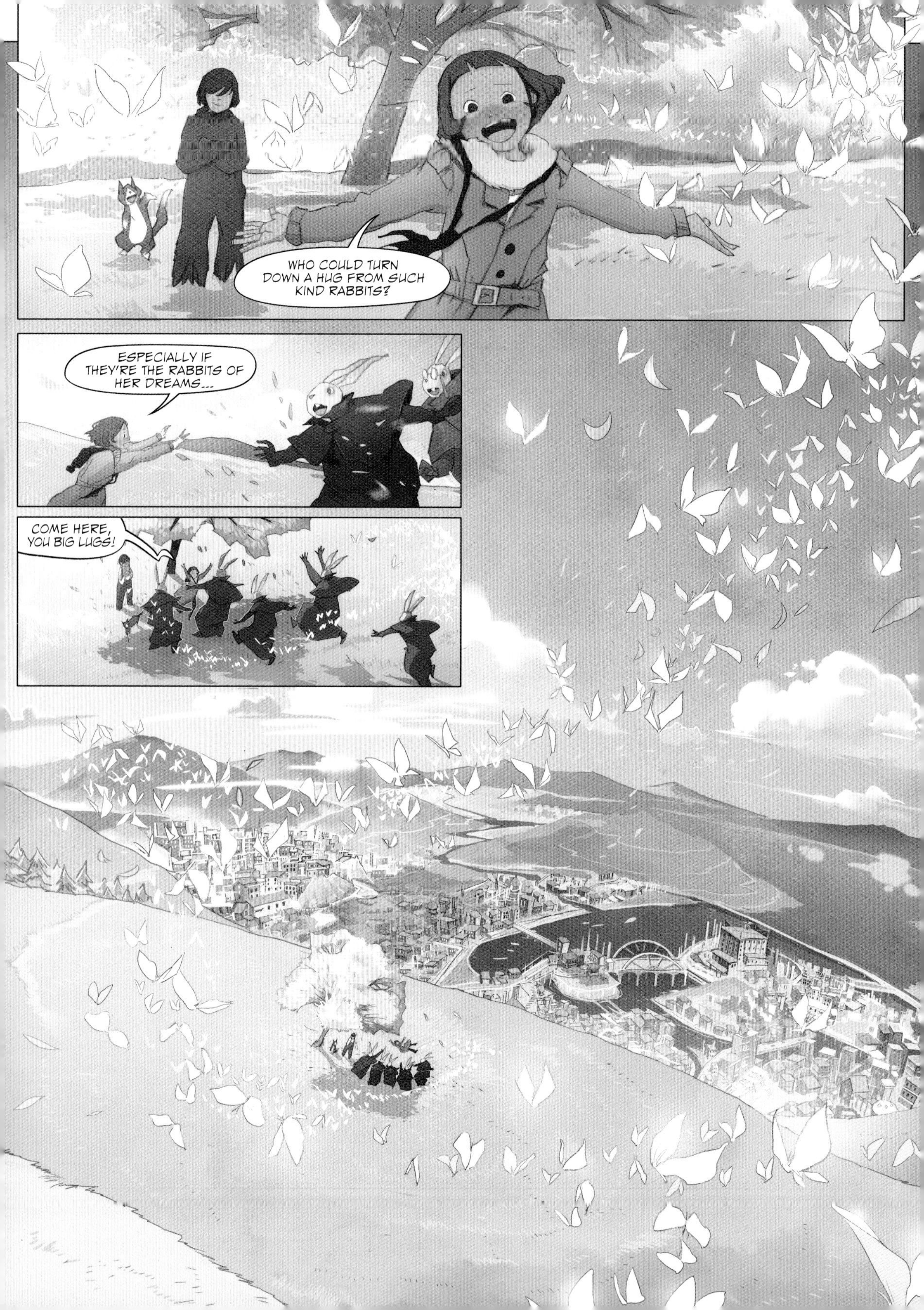
WHO COULD TURN DOWN A HUG FROM SUCH KIND RABBITS?
ESPECIALLY IF THEY'RE THE RABBITS OF HER DREAMS...
COME HERE, YOU BIG LUGS!

RICHARD MARAZANO

Richard Marazano is a French cartoonist and writer who studied physics and astrophysics before enrolling at the Fine Arts school in Angoulême. An accomplished comic artist in his own right, he is best known for his writing for other artists. He has written almost thirty books, including the multiple-award-winning series *Cuervos* and *The Chimpanzee Complex*.

LUO YIN

Luo Yin was born in Zhengzhou in the Chinese province of Henan. She graduated from the Beijing Film Academy with a specialization in animation in 2006. She worked as a freelance animator in Beijing for four years. She has also made illustrations for numerous magazines and children's books, including the Chinese and English bilingual children's book, *The Story of Little Penguin and Small Glacier.*